The Golden Calf

Henry Baum

First published in the United States of America
in 1997 as *Oscar Caliber Gun*
by Soft Skull Press

First published in Great Britain in 2000 by
Rebel Inc, an imprint of
Canongate Books Ltd, 14 High Street,
Edinburgh EH1 1TE

10 9 8 7 6 5 4 3 2 1

Rebel Inc series editor: Kevin Williamson
www.rebelinc.net

British Library Cataloguing-in-Publication Data
A catalogue record for this book is available on
request from the British Library

ISBN 0 86241 984 0

Typeset by Palimpsest Book Production Limited,
Polmont, Stirlingshire
Printed and bound in Great Britain by
Creative Print and Design, Ebbw Vale

The Golden Calf

FREDERICK HENRY BAUM was born June 29, 1972 in New York City and grew up in Los Angeles, California. He moved back to New York to get away from LA and he currently lives and writes in the Chinatown section of NYC. *The Golden Calf* is his first novel.

To Tim Griffith

Contents

1 I'm No One   1
2 Hand-Truck Drivers   11
3 The Last Straw   18
4 A Job in Security   26
5 Helen   34
6 Lambs with Wool Sweaters   42
7 The Ice-Cream Trucks   53
8 The Bottom of Things   58
9 Homeless Prom Night   64
10 The Proud and the Smug   73
11 Carl's Jr Star   81
12 God Doesn't Drive in a Limousine   89
13 Mr Out-of-touch   97
14 Canon Fodder   103
15 Happier than Hell   111
16 Dad   128
17 Devil's Advocate   137
18 Favorite Son   146
19 They   156
20 Never Let a Dog Piss on a Motorcycle   167
21 Hold Me in Your Charter Arms   177
22 .38 Caliber Performance   188
23 The End   196

Chapter One

I'M NO ONE

MARTA AND I met through her crazy fucking son, Robbie. It was kind of an accident really. But not really all that surprising. That son of hers was an accident waiting to happen. Her son was waiting outside my local liquor store and asking anybody and everybody to buy him a six pack of beer. It seemed that same night some drunk took off with his money after agreeing to get the beer for him. 'Wontcha do it?' the kid asked me. 'Some fag jetted with my money.' It was possible. There was a gay bar, the SS Happiness, close by. Robbie then told me there was an extra ten in it for me if I bought him the beer. I bought it for him. When I brought the beer to him he said, 'The money's at home. I'll give it to you when we get there.'

'When we get there?' I said.

He snorted, wiped his nose with his thumb and forefinger.

'I'm not going anywhere.'

'Please.'

I told the little kid to go away and drink his beer.

He said, 'I'll introduce you to my mother.'

'Your mother?'

'Sure.'

'What's your mother got to do with any of this?'

'She's sick in bed. I'm getting this for her.'

'Why's she drinking if she's sick in bed?' I asked.

'Just come over. I told you there's ten dollars in it for you.'

I didn't care much about the ten dollars. I just didn't have anything else to do. I had checked the TV page. There was nothing on. And the kid looked harmless enough. Pock-marked, but harmless.

On the way back to his house, he showed me a picture of his mother, a Polaroid. I'd never seen a Polaroid take a decent picture of anybody, so his mother wasn't very good looking. But that didn't matter. Ugly women knew what it was like to live. Pretty women didn't know anything about real life. They'd been looked at too long. Imagine, you're a mannequin, people staring at you your whole life, telling you how good you look and that's all that matters. You can't tell me that they know what it's like to really be alive. The uglier women had to rely on something other than their faces. So I felt something for them. And I was no one to complain. I wasn't all that pretty myself. And I hadn't had sex in over a year. I wasn't afraid to admit it.

Anyhow, pretty women scared me. That was true. They scared the hell out of me. Well, I'd say all women scared me, but it was the pretty women especially.

I stared at the picture. Underneath the woman's crooked expression like she was tasting something awful, and an ugly blouse covered with large orange flowers, I could see something desirable. Long, thick blond hair, and rough skin like it had some stories behind it, and a full woman body. I could see some of her in her son except that her son had wide, crazy eyes and you just couldn't look at anything but his nowhere stare.

We got to the house. It was white with light-blue trim, small, trapped between two apartment buildings. The house was over the garage. We climbed steep steps with chipped blue paint. He opened the door with a key. I followed him inside.

His mother wasn't sick. She greeted us at the door, a healthy red-faced glow. She was wearing a black dress that came just past her knees and a thin line of fake pearls, prettier than the photo-graph. She looked at me suspiciously. Her son, very businesslike, said, 'I got some beer,' like he was talking to his wife.

'Good,' she said and he went off into the kitchen. 'Who are you?' she asked. Her arms were crossed.

'I'm no one. Your son dragged me here.'

'Did you buy the beer for him?'

'Yes.'

'Thank you.'

There was a pause. Her son was watching us from the kitchen, peering at us with a wounded look.

'Does he do this a lot? Take people here?'

'Couple times.' She stopped, looked back at her son. His hands were curled around the door-frame, his head half hidden. 'The others didn't live to tell the tale.'

I think this was her idea of a joke. She barely smiled. It didn't lighten up the situation much. For a couple of seconds I thought she was serious and that feeling stayed. I just imagined the crazy son running out of the kitchen grasping a butcher knife and both mother and son robbing me blind. Their little private racket.

'Would you like to come in?' she said.

'Come in?'

'Yes, sit down.'

'Why?'

'Because you're here.'

It was fine reasoning. She looked at me sweetly then. She relaxed. Like her brain was tightening its muscle and then decided to smile.

'Fine, fine,' I said as if giving in after a great, long fight. 'I don't have much else planned.'

'Neither do I,' she said.

Funny how people meet each other. It always just falls into place, and comes at times when you've forgotten it's an option.

That night was the first and only time me and her slept together. It was awkward and slow, as if we were both virgins. I kept stopping in the middle because I thought her son was listening at the door. I heard soft scratching noises outside like a cat trying to get in. But I went ahead anyway. So Marta and I *screwed*. (My father once told me, 'You're not supposed to use a hammer on a screw, but that's the best way to do a woman.')

I never got the ten dollars from Robbie. He was a strange kid. Marta loved him. Eventually he started living at his father's house. He wanted to try a better life. His father was twenty years older than Marta, in his late fifties, and lived in a large house in the Hollywood hills. A high-priced lawyer. His name was Stewart and I met him only once, the day he took Robbie away. He shook my hand firmly, a real businessman's shake, and said hello and I never saw him again. Marta and him were married long enough to conceive a child. Now they rarely talked. He sent the monthly checks.

Marta and I had it fine. She saw other men, which left me alone a lot, but I had the TV to take care of me those times. There was nothing like the TV to wipe you out of loneliness. Alcohol and TV together? It was like you weren't even there.

I went over to Marta's maybe three times a week. Tonight was one of those nights. I usually walked there. It took about fifteen minutes. The good thing about walking to Marta's was the slight breeze of the ocean wafting over you. Those moments made it seem like LA had some clean air. We both lived by the beach, Venice. I lived in a small apartment, half underground, next to a parking garage. One small living room, a bedroom large enough to fit a bed and a small table, and a bathroom, cramped and plastic, like one you'd find in a Winnebago. Some people told me it was like living in a trailer.

The apartment was in the basement. The apartments upstairs were big and nice, with wooden floors, a full living room, separate kitchen and a large bedroom where you could walk around. I lived in the place the janitor was supposed to stay when they had a janitor living in the building.

Marta didn't live much differently. Same dirt-brown carpeting. Same thin, plaster walls. She lived at a busy intersection, across from an Italian restaurant and a laundromat. Hers was a sad house by design, small rooms, sagging walls. It wasn't much bigger than my apartment. But I had some good times there. She used to live in a much grander apartment, paid for by inheritance. Marta's family owned part of some small newspaper in the South. She used to have some money from her old-money grandmother's death that paid the rent on a house high in the Santa Monica hills. There was a big stained-glass window in the living room above an old marble desk with claws for legs. The stained glass lit the room colors of orange, blue and yellow. She would probably never have it that good again. Once the inheritance from the newspaper got thin, she and Robbie had to move to their small two-bedroom house.

I liked Marta in a long-term way. Marta was different from other people. She was good to me. Other people were only friendly to people they knew. Other people invaded the world and gave mean looks in my direction. Marta treated everybody like a nomad prince and her home was their own. Maybe that was why I got so close to Marta, she was something different. There was something serene about her, a waterfall compared to bullets. Most people ran cold and lukewarm, mostly cold. Marta always ran warm.

A couple of nights before, I had decided to let Marta know I liked her more than she thought. I wanted to make something more of what we had. I was tired of only smiling the times I saw her, smiling only once in a while. I wanted to always have it good.

I walked to her place, nervous but ready. I was usually never bold enough to make big moves so this was an important moment for me. But I knew I couldn't keep living my life the way I had been living it. Things had to change.

Marta greeted me at the door with an angry expression, the thin wrinkles by the sides of her eyes wrapped tight. She had complaint in her green-gray eyes. She stood like a barrier in the doorway and I almost thought she wasn't going to let me in. But she slackened, turned to the side, and let me pass.

The television was on high-volume in the living room. It was loud enough to be heard two houses over.

'Why don't you turn that down?' I asked.

'What. You mean the TV?'

'What else?'

'I was keeping it on while I did the vacuuming,' she said.

I looked down at the floor. The tan carpeting was covered with flecks of dirt and ash.

'You haven't been vacuuming,' I said.

'I haven't?' she said. She stared at me. Then she sucked at her first two fingers like they were holding a cigarette. She stared at her wet fingers for a good thirty seconds.

'Jesus, what the hell's the matter?' I said.

'News.'

'What?'

'I was watching the news.'

'Oh.'

That was enough like Marta. A little flighty sometimes. Small things affected her like death, but big things, like her own divorce, she just might smile and walk away.

Even so, I suspected there was something more wrong than the news.

'Something bothering you?' I asked.

'No. I'm just expecting a call.'

'A call? From who?'

'A man,' she said, slightly embarrassed.

That was all I needed to know.

She looked at the screaming TV as if for comfort. 'There's a war on, you know,' she said.

'There usually is.'

I walked over and turned the TV down, an old one with a curved dark-gray screen.

'Sit down, Ray. I'll be with you in a second.'

She walked hurriedly, flustered, into her bedroom.

The news was over. An entertainment show was on. An actor named Tim Griffith was saying how everything in his life was fabulous. That was the word he used: 'fabulous.' I didn't think I'd ever have the opportunity to describe my life that way.

'How's life, Ray?' someone might ask.

'I work at a warehouse, live in a basement. Everything's fabulous.'

That actor didn't know a thing about my warehouse, basement life. He never would.

Marta came back in looking sexier than I'd seen her in a while. She came out barefoot wearing a breezy-looking dress, a flower print. Most of the life and smile had come back to her face. The light from the kitchen bathed her in just the right kind of orange light.

'Do you want to see a movie?' she asked quickly, as if embarrassed to be looking so pretty.

'A movie?' I said.

'Yeah.'

'What movie?'

'There's a new Tim Griffith movie. I'm not sure what it's called.'

'Tim Griffith? I just saw him on TV.'

'Oh yeah?'

'Yeah. I don't know if I'd be interested in doing that.'

'No? That's too bad.'

I stared at Marta in her flower-print dress. The dress even smelled like flowers. It made her look soft all around. It kind of made me uneasy when she looked so good. Times like these I wanted to touch her. I had no idea how she'd react if I tried. When she looked good, it reminded me that she had a chance in the world, she had a natural fire. Unlike myself. Marta was going places. I thought maybe she could take me with her.

'You look good, Marta. Really good. Are you going out later or something?'

'No. I just bought it this week. I wanted to try it on. Do you like it?'

'Sure.'

'I think it makes my breasts look too big.'

'What's wrong with breasts being too big?' I said.

'Some men don't like that.'

'Not me.'

'Yeah, but you'd like a side of beef with a hole in it.'

I laughed politely, but that kind of hurt, coming from her. She just looked too good in that dress.

'So Marta, how about that guy who's going to call? Have you been dating anybody recently?' I put too much longing in my voice.

She came and sat by me on the couch.

'Saw a guy last Saturday as a matterafact,' she said.

'Yeah?'

'His name was Bill.'

'Bill, huh?'

'Yeah.'

'So – ah, did anything happen?'

'Sure,' she said and smoothed her dress against her pretty thigh. 'It all happened.'

'All what?' I said.

'I have to answer that?'

As if all my organs had turned black. 'What kinda guy is he?'

'He's in the music industry. He told me all about it but I wasn't really listening.' She got up and began walking around the room looking at the carpet, chewing her cheek like she did. A cute, concerned look that made her look younger than she was. 'He played with himself all through dinner under the table. He thought I couldn't see but I saw. One hand was holding the fork and the other was playing with himself.'

'And you went to bed with that kind of guy?'

'What can I say? He charmed me.'

'That's real pathetic, Marta.'

'Hey, what's with that?' she said and pointed a finger at me. 'I don't know. Maybe I felt a little sorry for him.'

'I feel sorry for you. You've done better than him.'

She began looking under books and magazines for her cigarettes.

'Take mine,' I said.

'Don't you want them?' she asked.

'I'm going to quit.'

'Yeah?'

'I'm going to try and turn my life around.'

'Really?' She just about shrieked. She was very surprised. 'That's good, Ray.'

She sat on the couch and took my cigarettes. She couldn't sit still and got up again. She was nervous about her bad new man. She went back to pacing, studying the dirty carpet.

'Marta, you've done better than that guy,' I said.

She didn't say anything.

'I'm better than him.'

'Probably are.'

'I've got a bad job, not like him, but I don't play with myself under the table.'

'Nope. You do that behind closed doors. You must get sick of masturbating all the time.'

She sat back down on the couch next to me and smiled yellow teeth. She kept whitening toothpaste in the bathroom but it didn't seem to work. I knew all her quirks, better than anybody. Goddamn, her breasts really did look better in that dress. She just embodied all the warm salvation women can be. I moved closer to her on the couch. She stayed where she was, staring at my box of cigarettes, turning it in her fingers like it was a tough puzzle. I put my hand on her back and rubbed gently. She made a small, calm smile. And then I did something very, very stupid. I lunged at her like I was trying to tackle her. But I missed the tackle and lost the game in the process. She cried out like I was a killer and ran into the bathroom.

I sat on the couch for the few minutes she was gone, staring at the dirty carpet. I was replaying the scene in my head like a terrible television sitcom where everyone booed instead of laughed. There was no way I could have done it better. I shouldn't have done it at all.

When she got out she said, 'Damn, Ray, we're not supposed to be doing that kind of thing anymore.' She was distraught, her eyes wide with a terrible look of fear and confusion.

I looked at my shoes, then to her. She looked prettier than before. Her face was flushed and red because she had washed it in the bathroom, washed me off of her. There was a splotch of water on her dress where she had spilled from the sink in the bathroom. She stood over me, hands on hips, reprimanding me, mother over son. Then she gave me a bad look of pity.

'Sorry,' I said.

'Sorry,' she said regretfully.

But she was right. Sometimes a person did get sick of masturbation.

Chapter Two

HAND-TRUCK DRIVERS

I LEARNED TODAY that I wasn't going to be anything. I was twenty-eight years old. I was reading about the Beatles today on the way to work. I got this encyclopedia that's supposed to have every fact about them. By the time those guys were twenty-eight they had done just about everything. They had changed the world. And they did something good. I watched other celebrities, like movie stars, and they had an air about them like they ruled the world. Now, I wasn't against success. I would have loved some of it. Some real world-changing success. What I didn't like was the no-talents or the almost-talents swallowing up success like junkies do drugs and then being rewarded for it. They were young and over-proud. I myself was twenty-eight years old. And that didn't mean a thing to anybody but me.

I worked in a warehouse. Somebody had to. Behind everything, there was people. They might have been happy people, sad people, rich people, or people who wanted to kill, but nothing worked by itself. When you walked outside and you saw the buildings, the streetlights, the trash on the street, you thought that it was a given, that was just the way things were. But that wasn't the case. The stuff had to be made by somebody. The M & M wrapper lying on the sidewalk had to be designed by some professional, then approved by someone higher, and then sealed up by a machine. People like me ran those machines. People like me somewhere else made those machines, and people somewhere else made the screws for the machines. There was a little life lesson for you. Things didn't make themselves. It was all made by people who had stuff on their minds.

I supposed that was the meaning of life right there. There was something behind everything. And behind that there's something else, down to the last atom. And nothing could ever be figured out because you keep going backward. You halve an atom, you just get half an atom. You halve that, you get a quarter, and so on. There was no way of figuring out what's behind it, what's behind anything.

That's not saying I didn't believe in God. I did. I just didn't believe in religion. Some kind of God had to exist to account for all the shit that happened. World War II was a perfect example. Most people said that was an example of how there wasn't a God. I said that the killing and the sadness that happened in that war was far too widespread to be put in people's hands. People weren't smart enough. It had to have been run by something else. It could have been God, or maybe the devil. But where there's a God there's a devil and where there's a devil there's a God.

That's what I was thinking about anyway, on the way to my job. On the way to a damp warehouse where I would lift boxes, mostly full of toys, for seven hours a day. I had had the job two years.

I walked in and I wasn't there a second before a man named Harry walked up to me. He was a short, gray, black man who looked like the kind of guy who would sit on the stoop of a building and shout his wisdom, even if no one was listening.

'You know, you're late,' he said.

'How's that? It's 9.30. We're supposed to be here at 9.30.'

'It's 10.30. It's daylight saving time.'

'Are you serious?'

'It's all right, though. A lot of guys were late. Even Walter was late.'

Walter was the boss.

'He's not mad is he?'

'Like I said, most guys were late.'

'Good.'

'Not like it's out of your style.'

'What do you mean? I'm never late.'

'Well . . .' he said and raised his eyebrows.

I didn't know what he could have meant. I was never late. Man, I hated that. People pointing a crazy finger at me as if I'd done something wrong and the whole problem all along is that they're the crazy ones.

The warehouse was a regular asylum. It was large and white like a hospital. The cement walls echoed all the bad jokes and the bad thoughts.

All the workers were standing around Walter's desk. I walked up and stood with them. Walter sat at a tan metal-countertop desk, the kind of desk where your elementary school teacher would sit at the front of the class giving lessons and orders. Which was exactly what Walter was doing.

There was an ashtray full to the brim by Walter's left arm. He hit the ashtray off the desk and it landed and wobbled like a Frisbee on the cold cement floor. Everybody moved out of the way and watched the ashes fall.

Walter ignored the ashtray. 'Shit, we've got a lot of work to do today,' he said. 'Who the hell invented this daylight saving thing anyway?'

'Well, Walt, it's because the sun—'

'That was a rhetorical Goddamn question.'

'Right.' The person he was talking to was named John, a wire-thin, pale guy as bland as his name. He probably still lived at home.

'You know what a rhetorical question is, John?'

'Well, yeah.'

'It's a question you're not supposed to answer, like what do you think of my wife.'

Some of the guys laughed. Partly to be polite, partly I thought because they were imagining his wife. I'd never seen her but I imagined her to be a real Edith Bunker type of a woman, wearing large-hipped dresses, cooking meatloaf, playing the piano she learned as a girl late at night.

Walter could have been on screen himself, playing the same part he was playing now, the touchy, old boss. He fit the part perfectly. He wasn't too bad-looking a guy. He had aged pretty well, kept all his hair, and had the gruff, gray hands and the screaming voice of the boss-stereotype they'd throw into a movie.

He was telling us the work that had to be done that day. 'Move five-six-one-eight to shipping. Six-six-oh-one and five-six-oh-four have to come back from the gate. Sorry about that.' The fifteen guys standing around the desk either listened to the boss or had quiet, laughing conversations of their own. I half-heard everything that was being said. I usually just walked in, walked out, and paid attention to no one. There wasn't any reason to listen. Everybody said the same things every day. Same routine information about boxes. Same unfunny bathroom jokes that always got big laughs. Sometimes the guys said I was too serious because I rarely laughed at the jokes. 'You should smile more,' they said, which people had said to me all my life and crawled deep under my skin. 'Ray, you're an old man before your time.' My silent reply was, 'Am I too serious or is everybody else just not very funny?' I'd glare and glare and hope they'd get my point.

Walter told me that my job today was to load the boxes on to the forklift that had mistakenly been taken to the shipping gate the day before. 'Six-six-oh-one and five-six-oh-four, you got that?' he screamed at me, as if to a child.

'I think I can handle it,' I told him.

I went to my station and started working.

I had a serious and constant disdain for my co-workers but I did the job with some degree of faithfulness. Although it was a job that was hard to do poorly. I just lifted the boxes on to the forklift, around the warehouse, or to trucks that would take the boxes to stores or other warehouses.

John and Harry were standing next to me talking about their

wives. Together they were lifting a solid, heavy box full of dinosaur toys that had just arrived cross-country on a long truck. I could predict what they were going to say before they even opened their mouths.

'Hey, John, how's your wife.'

Shut up, man, you know I'm divorced.

'Shut up, man, you know I'm divorced.'

'I thought I saw her last night.'

You did, where?

'You did? Where?'

Some easy insult.

'On the strip. I think she got arrested for prostitution.'

They would both laugh. 'Shaddup, you fuck.' HA-HA.

I didn't need to listen to anyone. Listening to my own thoughts was more interesting.

Although lately those thoughts were getting louder and more hateful than usual. More urgent, more like they were controlling themselves. You know how it is to be angry, to be in an argument with someone, the thoughts of what you're going to say next just rush into your head involuntarily, and you just pick and choose which insult you want to throw out next. My sad, cynical head was making the decisions for me. 'Ray,' my mind told me, 'this is all bullshit, you're swimming in bullshit.' Part of me didn't want to believe this was true, I still held on to a bit of optimism. I might have spit bitter all the time but that was because I had hope about how things should be. But then my mind would say, Give in, Ray, I'm right, we're fucked. I supposed my mind's voice was helping me deal with life's trials as best it could. Goddammit it though if sometimes it was making life harder for me. Sometimes I didn't agree with the choices it made. Like I'd be standing at a stoplight and this little voice would tell me to cross against the light, right into the onslaught of speeding cars. 'That's not right,' I'd say. Still, something upstairs wanted me to take the step. Lately it seemed that something else inside me was picking its own side of the argument and telling me what was right and wrong. Lately I was feeling like I was having an argument with something inside me more and more.

I didn't think I was crazy, I thought everybody else was. Walter with his forty years without pension working in the warehouse, Marta and her bad men, just a general malaise smog that had settled on the city of Los Angeles. The voice in my mind said the people I worked with were wrong, they took themselves too seriously. They might have called me serious but they were the ones who took a sad amount of pride in such easy, mindless work. The other guys lifted the boxes with some kind of grim satisfaction. They made jokes and moved boxes like working at the warehouse was a life sentence. I knew there had to be something else out there to keep me occupied and fed, with rent paid and satisfied, I just hadn't found it yet. So I was biding my time moving boxes or driving the lift across the dirty warehouse floor.

I used the forklift to pick up the boxes and I brought them to different areas in the warehouse. From there, I picked up the boxes by hand and stacked them in the right place. They were heavy but I lifted them with both arms. Sometimes I stacked two on top of each other. My arms were getting stronger. The tan, cardboard boxes were filled with movie star plastic men, dinosaurs, Transformers, dolls that cried when you squeezed them, waterguns that shot fifty feet, stuff I wouldn't have dreamed of when I was a kid. No sugar cereals, no ice cream after dinner unless the report card was just right, no toys with small parts that I could choke on. Every little kid's nightmare. Mom said. Of course, the best toys always had the smallest parts. The toys I lifted for work now were heavy and expensive, complex and detailed, assembly required. They were toys that kids would get as a gift on a birthday, or nag their moms about at the toy store, maybe the kids would cry. They would do anything so they could get the toys I lifted day to day. When the kids finally opened the packages they would scream in an ecstasy of gratitude and be happy for a couple of weeks.

The day went on like every other regular day.

When I was walking out of the warehouse something happened. I saw a celebrity, Robert De Niro. I didn't know what he was doing out of New York. And I had no idea what he was doing around these warehouses. There were a couple of restaurants nearby, but that was it. Maybe he was checking out a location for a new movie. The people around the area were excited, gawking at him like the new imported panda at the zoo. The man had poise and confidence. People were all over him, asking for autographs, asking questions like they were reporters, and he calmly shook his head and answered with things he'd probably said a thousand times before. I envied that. Such grace. Such importance. Even out here among the warehouses, the workers' desert, he was plagued by people wanting him.

Just then, tall, pale John came out. When he saw De Niro he must have regressed to about ten years old. He began jumping up and down like a kid wanting something and he started screaming about how he loved all of his movies. De Niro noticed this guy's crazy enthusiasm and pulled back a little, holding up his hand like a stop sign. John didn't pay this any mind and moved in closer, even patting De Niro on the back. Fucking moron. De Niro briskly walked away and the crowd dispersed. Everybody left except John who followed him to the corner where De Niro turned and disappeared. John lingered at the corner, pacing. Give the guy some space, I thought. This guy is better than you'll ever be. He doesn't care about you. You might see his movies. He might play a guy who works in some warehouse. But when he's walking through warehouses he could give a shit about the real people inside. He might work in a warehouse for a week or two as research, but when it comes to the real hand-truck drivers, he could give a shit. John, just leave the man alone.

Chapter Three

THE LAST STRAW

A COUPLE OF days later I called in sick to work. I decided to go over to Marta's to straighten out what I'd messed up the last time I saw her. I liked Marta. I wanted to keep what we had. Maybe I could make something better of it. I still had a small dream that she could take me away from the bitterness.

I walked up the steep stairs and opened the door. The door was usually unlocked. When I walked into Marta's apartment I heard moaning. It wasn't coming from Marta. It was deeper, eerie, like the moans that would come from a ghost. They didn't sound like the moans of sex, but I was wrong. I walked through the living room to Marta's room. The moans were loud now, still ghost-like. I opened the door to Marta's room. The door had one dying flower stapled to the outside. In the room, a man, a tan man, a man with a thin film of fuzz on his back and legs, was doing Marta from behind. His eyes were closed, his head lifted to the air, and he was making those strange sounds to the ceiling as if he were calling to the Gods. Marta had her face straight in the pillow so I couldn't see her, but she was clutching the pillow fiercely with both hands like she could have been feeling pleasure or pain.

Neither of them saw me at first. I was about to leave with the vivid still-frame photograph of the scene in my head. But the two of them shocked me into saying, 'I'll just wait outside.'

The guy looked over at me, still moaning, and widened his eyes in fear, and then for some reason he began pumping faster. He kept on staring at me. I guess I did look pretty frightening. I wasn't looking my best. I was wearing a dark-green trench coat and black shoes almost worn to the toe and I probably had close to the same look of fear that he did.

I left fast and closed the door with a slight slam, just enough to let them know that I was there and I didn't like them. I went into the living room, sat on the couch, and just thought. Sex could ruin a person. People liked sex because they liked to be ruined. For a half hour or whatever it took, they'd commit suicide, vacant, sweaty, and masochistic.

Marta came out looking like what I'd described. She looked just as vacant. She was in a white robe and was so covered with sweat she looked like she had just gotten out of the shower. One breast was about to fall out of her half-open robe. And she was having trouble breathing, as if she'd just walked in the door after running a marathon.

'How long have you been here?' she asked.

'Long enough.'

She looked regretful.

'Is that the music industry guy?'

'Yeah.'

She was still high from sex, I could tell. She looked how anyone looks on some drug, eyes glazed over, smiling a little as if out of shame.

'What's his name?'

'Bill,' she whispered as he came out.

He stood next to her. Our eyes locked and he stared at me coldly like a cop to a criminal.

'I'm Ray, if you're interested.'

'Ray.'

'And you're Bill.'

'I'm Bill.'

'That's what she said.'

He didn't say anything. He didn't move. Nobody did. I looked at Marta, sadly I think, because this was a sad scene. I was sitting on the couch, my hands in my lap, and the two of them towered above me like a big, menacing suicide cliff.

I had to say something. 'So I hear you're in the music business,' I said. It was a stupid thing to say. But anything would have sounded stupid, considering.

'Who are you?' he said, dead-voiced.

'I'm a friend of Marta's.'

'You're not . . .' He shook his head in a yes motion and opened his eyes wide.

'I'm not what?'

'You're not her boyfriend?'

'What – you think I'm her, no – and I bet you thought I was going to hurt you for it.'

'Well, you know, a man walks in and one thinks.'

'No,' I laughed slightly. 'I'm just Ray.'

Things loosened up then. As much as they could. Marta said, 'I'm glad you two finally get to meet.' But, naturally, she wasn't. Not like this.

After our introductions were complete I finally got a good look at him. He was sickly, this guy. Even if they hadn't just gotten done having sex he would have been sweating. He was all hair, tan, balding pretty severely in a straight line across his head, and he was wearing a gold chain. I tell you, that was what made me hate him right away, a gold fucking chain. He had cocaine and money written all over him.

I felt sorry for Marta. I didn't know why she ever went out with guys like him. A man who looked like that could never treat her right. Most times you could judge a person by the company they kept, but somehow I still liked Marta.

'What are you doing here, Ray? Why aren't you at work?' Marta asked.

'I called in sick. I thought you and me could do something.'

'Not today, Ray,' she said and glanced at Bill.

'No, looks like you've got other things to do.'

'Some other time.' She said that like it would be never again.

This blew my day off, and any hopes for me and Marta.

I got up and made a great groan as if it was causing me pain to move. I wanted her to know I felt something, something very raw, something like angry regret. She stood by the couch with Bill, nervously scratching her back with one hand.

I stopped at the door. Insults started washing over my brain like they had been lately. That little voice, almost as high-pitched as a child's, took me over without letting me choose what I was going to say. I said, 'I wish I was your boyfriend so I could have good reason for kicking the shit out of Bill here. I normally don't like Bills,' I looked at Marta. I couldn't have stopped if I wanted. She and Bill were both perfectly still. 'I don't like paying my bills. Most bills that get passed by the government tend to fuck up the country. I guess this Bill here is no exception.' Then I paused. 'Fuck the two of you.'

Marta was about to raise her hand to say something. Bill was expressionless. He still hadn't moved a muscle like the sweat-dumb industry type that he was. I moved away quickly before they could say a word. I walked out the door and slammed it lightly, angry but controlled.

I smiled as I walked down the steps. That felt good. I loved that feeling. I just really gave it to someone and all they could do was sit there puzzled, feeling bad for having done me any harm. I hoped they felt some guilt. Guilt for fucking with me and guilt for living their cold-shoulder lives.

But as I walked along further, in no direction in particular, I began to feel wrong. They wouldn't feel any guilt. That's why I hated their kind in the first place. If Bill felt any guilt or shame he wouldn't have been wearing that gold chain. No one who had any decency about them would wear a gold chain. He was lost. He didn't feel any regret about anything.

And Marta? She was all right, I guess, but she was corruptible.

I felt a little bad for making her feel any worse than she was already feeling. I knew Marta. She had her problems. And she must have been feeling exceptionally low to jump in her bed with Bill. Twice. Probably more than that. I didn't want her sad.

So as I walked on I felt as if I'd blown my chance. I had an opportunity to prove to Marta that I was something real, something better, someone she could be with. But I had fucked up again. My moment in the sun had shattered into a thousand tiny fragments of flame, singeing my brain and falling off my body like sweat. I walked down the street burning like a fire, giving off the heat of failure.

At that point there was nothing to do but call and say I'd be coming in to work. I went over there and worked for an hour but then my arms started hurting. My arms were tensing up. The sides of my arms felt like the muscles were pushing through the skin. I didn't think I could last the day with all those thoughts about Marta and Bill on my mind.

On my lunch break, I sat alone in a corner eating a bologna sandwich out of a paper bag. I hid behind old boxes of toys we rarely shipped. I looked at the boxes of toys and wondered about them. Marta made me feel like a child, like a disruptive kid who walked in on his parents having sex. In one of those boxes in the back of the warehouse there was a set of *Star Wars* toys. I had been too old for *Star Wars* when it came out and I felt I'd missed out. I envied all the younger kids who played with all those new toys, bragged about getting the Death Star, or the Millennium Falcon. I wanted to play with those kids, and I would have, but I was thirteen when all that hit and the other kids at school would have lynched me. There was a kid a year younger than me, Leslie Rawling, who played with all kinds of toys. It was bad enough that his parents had to give him a girl's name, he also got teased for playing with toys. So I wasn't about to go play with them. I could only watch the younger kids and imagine.

But now, at the age of twenty-eight, almost twenty-nine, hidden behind the tall stacks of boxes, I could do anything I wanted.

I opened a box labeled 'Star Wars' and went inside. I lined up the good-guy figures on one side of the floor and removed some of the bad guys. I hit the figures lightly together, tentatively. Their outstretched arms hit each other as if slowly fighting. Maybe I was crazy. But I was enjoying myself. It was almost like a form of meditation. Cardboard packages lay ripped open all about me.

It got my mind off everything. People had no idea the crazy stuff I did when I was alone. Watching TV for twelve hours straight, peering out the window endlessly and watching the pedestrians, writing anonymous letters to strangers out of the phone book. I could do anything I wanted. There was something nice about doing it in public.

'You can't do that. I'll avenge the murder of Leia,' I said, quietly. I didn't want anyone to hear me. Then Darth Vader and Skywalker fought. Darth Vader was winning, his legs on top of Luke Skywalker, when I heard the shuffling of feet nearby. I gathered all the toys together and threw them into the box. Then I stashed the box under and behind others so it couldn't be found.

'Who's there?' somebody asked. 'Is anybody there?' It was Walter, the boss.

I came out from behind the boxes and found Walter staring at me. He was wearing his standard short-sleeve white button-down shirt and wide, brown pants. Walter was a fat man. A soft fat like from huge, happy feasts. Now he was frowning.

'What you doing back there?'

'Nothing.'

'Nothing, huh? A person should never be doing nothing. I never like a person to be doing nothing.'

I said, 'I thought I saw a rat. I mean I did. I saw a rat and I wanted to kill it.'

'We have traps for that.'

'I know. But see, this rat's been getting on my nerves. It's been bugging me lately. I wanted to kill it once and for all.'

'You've got something against this particular rat?' he said.

'Yeah. It's got a black streak on its back so I know it's the same one.'

'It's a little war, you say?'

'Yeah.'

'Man on rat.' He chuckled big.

'Yeah, like that. I've been after it for a while.'

'I can understand it. But let me tell you this,' suddenly very serious. 'I never, repeat never, want to see you doing nothing.'

'OK, Walter.'

He stared at me.

'Sir,' I said.

He continued staring and then said, 'All right. I've got a job for you now.'

He laid out the details for moving fifty boxes of lifelike baby-dolls to shipping.

One thing I could do well was lie. It was second nature. That thing about the rat came easy. Though it wasn't entirely a lie. There was a rat I'd been after for a couple of weeks. I really thought they avoided the traps. I'd never seen one caught.

When Walter left I went right back to the *Star Wars* toys. It wasn't as much fun now knowing that someone might be around. Knowing I could get caught. But still I went ahead. Darth Vader was about to kill Leia, Luke Skywalker, and Han Solo in one fight. I didn't get far before I glanced up and saw Walter looking down at me. His head peeked over the boxes like Godzilla over city buildings.

'How long have you been there?' I asked him.

'Long enough.'

I was sitting Indian-style, movie toys around me in a circle.

'I don't like this shit, Ray.'

'I'm just trying to relax.'

'Relax, huh?'

'Yeah.'

'This is some crazy shit.'

'I'll put them away.'

I started throwing the toys as fast as I could into the tall cardboard box.

'It's not just this. You know, I've been wondering about you, Ray. You've been here two years and you do the job, but I've been wondering about you.'

'For what?'

'For one thing, you never talk to anyone.' He stamped a cigarette out on the cold, cement floor.

'I have friends outside.'

'That's fine, but I don't like this kind of crazy shit going on in the warehouse.'

'I won't do it again.'

'But, you see, you already have some warnings I haven't told you about. Eating your lunch alone, for one. I want my people to get along.'

'Sorry.'

'Well,' he said. The way he said that one word, letting out a long deflated breath, was as final as anything. 'I'd have to say this is the last straw,' he said.

'The last straw?'

'Yes.'

'I'm fired?'

'You're fired.'

Chapter Four

A JOB IN SECURITY

WELL, WHAT THE hell, I needed another job. Nothing all that new. Someone had told me that being a security guard was the easiest job to get. They didn't check résumés. They didn't care who you were, even if you had a prison record. I didn't have a record but I didn't have a clean résumé either. I'd been fired from too many jobs. I worked as a dishwasher before I worked at the warehouse. I left that job somewhere between being fired and quitting. The boss, Jake, caught me staring at another boss named Molly. He said he didn't like the way I was looking at her. But, you know, in a job you've got to stop and look around sometimes to keep yourself from going mad, and you get spaced out and lose your stare. I started looking at Molly. I mean she was pretty and if you're going to look at something it might as well be her, and by the time Jake saw me my eyes weren't even in focus. He took that unfocused stare that people get as lust and he took me in the corner and reprimanded me about it.

'I don't want you looking at Molly, hear me?' he said.

'I wasn't, I was just—'

'If I ever catch you looking at her that way again, you're fired.'

I had the feeling that he wanted Molly himself and he didn't want me there as competition. That made me glad.

But since the time he talked to me, he wouldn't stop watching me. Every time I took a rest from working, and started looking around, I'd catch Jake staring at me from somewhere in the kitchen. I couldn't stand it. Jake took away the freedom of my eyes. That was something I needed more than anything. So I quit.

I definitely couldn't use that job as a reference. It seemed that most jobs I took had something negative attached to them, so I either quit or got fired and couldn't use the reference.

I looked in the paper under 'Security' and found plenty. There were a whole bunch for warehouses, but I wanted to stay away from that, and a couple others for office buildings, but that sounded stale. Then there was one for a college. That sounded right. And they probably paid the most too. Parents would shell out a whole lot to protect their sons and daughters. I called them up and set up an appointment for an interview. They asked if I had any experience. I told them I had been a security guard at the warehouse I'd just been fired from. If they called and found me out, I'd just move on. Maybe they'd call and ask, 'Did Ray Tompkins work for you from August '91 to May '93?' They'd say yes and that would be done.

To make a long story short, I got the job. I could tell you all about going over there and having the interview and almost tripping over myself when I asked, 'Do you get to carry a gun?' The interviewer, pale, with forty-year-old acne, frowned. But he brightened when I said, 'The reason I want this job is because I want to be close to learning.' But I won't tell you the rest of it because I hate interviews. Painful as anything. Like your own thirty-second commercial.

My first day at the job was interesting enough.

A man named Bud showed me around the campus. I said, 'Hey, Bud, how you doing?' I laughed and said again, 'Hey, Bud,' but I don't think he understood what I was driving at. He said, 'I'm fine, why do you ask?' in the most confused way.

Bud was a short, ghost-white man who looked like he had lost a lot of weight recently. He didn't look healthy thin. He looked weak and tired. He had a brittle voice, as if overcooked.

The campus was small and easy to take care of. The school was right in the middle of a wealthy suburb so there wasn't much threat from the outside. True, I'd heard of murders occurring at these quiet schools, but it didn't look like anything could happen here. The place looked too nice, too serene. All the well-cut, golf-course lawns, ivy falling off the buildings like water off a woman just out of the shower. Even a murderer would turn away out of respect.

I liked it there. I could tell already. My job, Bud told me, was to patrol around in one of the maroon station-wagon security cars with the name of the college written on the side, and help students who were locked out of their dorms, or transport someone from one dark spot to another, or look out for prowlers. Probably I wouldn't be doing that much at all.

Bud said that there were so many little things that always needed to be done that I would just have to learn as I went along. There was no sense in training me. I knew how to unlock a door, right?

'That's all you need to know,' Bud said. 'Think you can handle it?'

Bud looked me up and down like I couldn't chew my food.

'Yes.'

He wiped his nose with his fingers and ran the snot through his hair. 'It's easy. Let's get you a uniform.'

He unlocked a padlock on a tall locker and handed me a uniform. The uniform was a gray-blue shirt and pants with the name of the school embroidered over the heart. It looked more or less like a gas station attendant's uniform. The uniform would easily separate me from the students' expensive sweaters and fashionable pants.

'Now here's a skeleton key. It can open every door in the college.'

He looked at me.

'I know what a skeleton key is,' I said.

'What?' he yelled as if I had talked back.

'Sorry.'

'Sorry? What are you sorry for?'

That was Bud.

'Don't ever lose this key. If you lose this key, we've got problems. It would be bad news if this key got into the wrong hands. You hear me? This can open everything. Computer center. Girls' dorm rooms. Everything.'

He stopped and blinked hard as if he had made a silent, imperceptible sneeze.

'Here's your night stick for, you know, whatever happens. I heard that you asked if we carried a gun. We don't.'

'I was joking.'

'What?'

'About the gun. I was joking.'

'That's nothing to joke about,' he said seriously but went on. 'Here's a flashlight for later at night. Keys to the car. Here's a map of the school. There's first aid in this drawer if you need it. You know how to work a Band-Aid?'

'Yes.'

'OK.'

'I don't know CPR.'

He thought that over.

'That's OK. Neither do I.'

I put the skeleton key, along with other keys to the parking lot deadbolts, on my key chain with the keys to my apartment and my car.

'Anything ever happen here?' I asked.

'What?'

'Anything really bad ever happen?'

'The worst I've seen since I've been here, and I've been here twenty-five years, is an old pervert who used to come around and hassle the girls and hand out some lewd writing of his that he'd xeroxed. Once he flashed a girl. We tracked him down and threatened him with a lawsuit and he never came back. Sometimes he sends us his writings through the mail. He still lives in town because that's where the postmark's at. Aside from that, nothing's really happened. We've been fortunate that way. Kids get violent sometimes, but you know, that's a given.'

We didn't say anything for a little while.

'That's it,' he said.

'What should I do now?'

'I don't know,' he said. 'Just ride around awhile until we call you for something.'

Just like that. I had a job.

The job was easy. Aside from letting teachers and students into buildings there wasn't very much to do except patrol around.

One of the problems with the job was that, like a restaurant job, I had to work weekends. And because I was new, those were the shifts they were more willing to give me.

I didn't make friends with the other guards. I didn't want to. Like the warehouse workers, they were over-devoted. It always saddened me to see people devoting themselves to something of such low purpose. Guys at the warehouse would place a box so it'd fit just right, parallel to the painted lines on the warehouse floor. The other guards patrolled around with their eyes peeled like owls. They'd open a door as if they were opening a vault of jewels. Nothing angered me so much as misplaced devotion. I stayed away from them.

Bud I liked all right. At sixty, there was nowhere else he *could* go, so I wasn't going to fault him for it.

My first week on the job I had to work the Monday I got hired through Saturday. Saturday, the campus was emptier than I expected. Most of the students went into LA to have a night in the wide, flat, forbidding city. I wasn't sure what I thought about the students yet. For the most part they seemed pale and uninteresting. The tan ones were less interesting, and they were the ones who threw parties at night. I couldn't believe I was only seven years older than them. I felt like an old man. Some of the students looked fresh out of puberty, flat-chested, thin teenage mustache, awkward and unformed, not very attractive. The youngest students were the ones who tried to talk to me. They hadn't learned shame enough yet to know to leave the security guard alone. They'd say things to me like, 'Hey, Ray, pretty nice day, isn't it?' I'd grunt back and they'd go away smiling like they did a service. They'd probably tell their friends excitedly, 'I talked to Ray, that new security guard.' Proud that they were talking to the underclass. Their young, naive faces would consider me like homework. I was a mystery to them.

I guessed anyone with a job like mine, a job full of empty busywork, tough on the heart and head because it could get so boring, was a mystery to them.

A couple of the students I liked and I talked to them. They were the quiet few, always alone, and they wouldn't have said a word to me if I hadn't said something to them first. I bet those kids would one day be famous. They were the smart ones. You could tell they were smart because they sheltered themselves away. Those were the students I felt like protecting, people who were awkward since birth.

Saturday night, one of the dorms threw a party. I'd seen about three of these parties since I started working there. They always had a sad feel about them, a feel of kids trying to be adults. These lost, lonely child-adults roamed around half-smiling, trying to talk to one another. But where at a cocktail party the talking was soft and controlled, the students would shout, cower away, cover their mouths and look to the ground. I watched from the sidelines. Most of the security guards watched the parties like watching a television episode. Carl, a short, black security guard with gray sideburns, said, 'She sure is hot, isn't she?' about a thin blond girl straight out of the pages of a teenage swimsuit issue. 'Wouldn't mind me soma that.' The more confident kids went off and had sex. They were usually the ones who made the most trouble; they were confident enough to be a nuisance. Young and rowdy, they were learning how to be bad men and women in later life.

At about 9.00 I got a call to shuttle four girls from the parking lot furthest from campus to the dorm named 'Hirschfeld' where the party was being held. When I got there all four girls were huddled together, holding their bare arms in the summer night cool. They looked cold and afraid. Many of the girls at the school were pretty. Some of them looked right out of junior high school, but some others looked mature enough that they could pass for twenty-five. These four girls were a mix of old and young. They all piled into the back seat of the car. One by one they shyly said, 'Hi,' as if by obligation.

When they got in they started talking like birds, as if happy to finally be warm inside and they could do as they pleased. 'I'm glad we're doing this,' said one of the girls.

'It's not like we have a choice.'

'It's not safe anywhere.'

'Did you know Ken got beat up when he walked into town?'

'Who's Ken?'

'He used to be Jason.'

'He changed his name to Ken?'

'Yeah.'

'Why?'

'For the theatre.'

I looked into the rear-view mirror. Three of the girls were talking, but one was silent, staring at the back of the front seat. She didn't seem to be hearing a word. I liked her right off.

She was wearing a dark-gray, hooded sweatshirt with the sleeves cut off. She had a dark complexion and darker eyes. She peered out from the hood and saw me looking at her in the rear-view mirror. I looked away.

'I don't know if I want to go to this party,' this girl said.

'Why not?'

'I just have a feeling about it.'

'You can leave if you want, Helen,' said one of the other girls impatiently.

We were there. A two-minute walk. A two-minute drive with all the stoplights. The lights were meant to slow suburban drunk drivers. They got out of the car and all quietly said, 'Thank you.' I replied loudly, 'You're welcome, girls,' as if to make up for their shy quiet. The girl in the gray hood was a little louder than the rest and she gave me a short look in the rear-view mirror.

All I knew about her was what I saw right there, but I knew I liked her. She seemed thoughtful in a way the others weren't. Like she had been let in on some privileged information and she was staying quiet about it. And she had a name like Helen, a real old-time name. It wasn't any gutless, young name like Becky or Kelly. You couldn't grow up with a name like Helen without learning something. Just like ugly women, a person learned something from imperfection. She wasn't part of the Heathers and the Jennifers. She was on her own. Marta was the same way, but she'd already fallen over to the other side. Helen was still young, too young to be tainted. There was something more to Helen. I could tell. There was something real. I wanted to find out all about it.

Chapter Five

HELEN

SUNDAY I HAD off so I decided to visit Marta. I should have learned from the last time not to go over unexpectedly, but I had an old-habit urge to see her. Cocaine and gold-chain Bill was there when I arrived.

'Hi, Ray. Long time,' Marta said when she closed the door behind me. She had on a forced smile.

I stared at Bill. He sat on the couch, legs spread wide apart.

'He was just leaving,' Marta said, which may or may not have been true.

'Oh yeah?' I said.

'I have to go to work,' Bill explained, as if he needed a reason to go because he felt he belonged there.

I sat down in a dining room chair. The dining room was just a table in the corner of the living room. I sat with my back to Bill. I wasn't going to say a word until he left.

I heard him get up. I could see him out of the corner of my eye.

'I'll call you when I get back to work,' he said to Marta quietly.

'OK,' Marta whispered.

'You have a good day.' He glanced at me.

'Thank you. I will,' Marta whispered again. She didn't want me to hear. The exchange was almost as private and intimate as sex. I couldn't help but listen.

'Bye,' Marta said breathily.

'Bye,' Bill said. 'Be good.'

'How've you been?' Marta asked me when the door closed, after she had whispered something inaudible to Bill and taken his earlobe temporarily into her mouth.

'I've been fine,' I said. I couldn't work up eye contact. 'I have a new job.'

'You do? What happened to the warehouse?'

'I got fired.'

'Oh. Why?'

'I work as a security guard at a college now.'

'That's good work,' she said.

'It is.'

'Come to think of it, I may be getting a new job too.'

'Oh yeah?'

'Bill,' she coughed, 'may be able to get me a job as a receptionist at a music company.'

'Well, that's a step up. A receptionist at a doctor's office to a receptionist at a music company.'

She didn't flinch. 'The pay's better.'

'One heals, the other kills.'

'Goddamnit, Ray. Now I remember how great it is to see you.'

There wasn't all that much sarcasm in her voice. She was never very good at sarcasm.

There was quiet. Marta looked restless, like she didn't want me to be there.

'So, how are you and Bill?' I asked after I couldn't stand it anymore.

'He's fine,' she said.

'You guys taking any blood tests soon?'

She scoffed. 'He's clean, Ray.'

'I meant for marriage.'

'Marriage? We aren't going to get married.'

'Why not?' I asked.

'Because it's not that way.'

'You sure?'

'Jesus. I feel like a mother telling her kid about her new boyfriend.'

'I'm just curious.'

'We just have a good time together.'

'I've heard that before.'

Just then I thought about all the good times I'd missed. Not just with Marta, not just sex, but everything. Marta's life was basically a waste, but she was having a good time. Anyone could waste away a life, that was easy, but it was tough to enjoy it. It was so tough to smile in the devil face of boredom and restlessness. Tough to find other people who might help you enjoy yourself.

'Yeah, we have a good time,' Marta repeated. 'Just the other day we went to the pier and Bill jumped off the end in all his clothes. All of the old fishermen thought he was crazy. A couple people thought it was a suicide. I was just laughing. I met him under the pier and then we, well, and then . . .' she stopped and paused.

'Jumped off the pier, you say.'

'Yes,' she said, relieved. 'So are you seeing anyone?'

I thought about Helen, about her small twenty-one year old face tucked behind that gray sweatshirt. I thought about the next time I'd see her.

'Ray?' Marta asked again. I must have been sitting there for some time in silence.

'I've met someone,' I said.

'Oh, yeah?' she said, excited. 'Who?'

'She wears . . . sweatshirts.'

'Sweatshirts?'

'Yeah. You'd like her.'

I left Marta's feeling all right. I should have been feeling pretty poor because of the situation with Marta and Bill, but I felt fine. I thought about Helen and I thought about the future. I walked down the cracked, gray sidewalk back to my apartment, my heels actually kicking in the air. Maybe things wouldn't be so bad for me after all.

I was eager to get back to the job. The following week was more boring than usual. I had lost the initial enthusiasm I had for the job when I first got there. More than once I stopped working completely. I stopped the patrol car and stared at the lawns and the rich, green trees surrounding the houses near the campus. A world surrounded by trees, caught in the glass bubble shroud of the sky. A human fishbowl. There could be hours when there was nothing for me to do, nobody was calling me in. I spent a lot of time watching the students walking among the red-brick buildings, smiling or serious. Of course, there were jobs I could have been doing. I could have been check-ing if various doors were securely locked or I could patrol around and see if anybody needed anything. But after a while I found that the doors were almost always locked and if somebody really needed me, they'd call. So, sitting alone among the fine trees, I'd think. Mainly I'd think about Helen. I wanted to get her last name so I could send her a note in her mailbox. Nothing serious, just something to say there was somebody out there who wanted to meet her. She was a different breed than me but I got the sense from that one night that she wanted to learn about something else, something real, away from the green trees and pretty-pretty smiles.

Sometimes I saw her walking around campus. She was one of the serious students, head down, muscles tight, almost as if she were always cold. She usually wore that same gray sweatshirt. Other times she'd wear old T-shirts, worn thin. She was too smart to care about fashion. Another thing I liked about her.

I wasn't thinking too seriously about her. I mean, she was a student and I'd get fired for getting involved, but also she looked like she was in need of something, some kind of reinforcement, and I wanted to help her.

I didn't know how I was going to get her name. I couldn't ask one of her friends. I thought about coming up with a fake poll to find out if students were interested in starting their own security program on campus, and then just ask her last name. But she might see through that. And I didn't know if I could face her. I didn't know what to do. But then I realized something. I was security. I had access to everything. Problem was, I had all the keys in the world but I couldn't work the school computers. So I asked the secretary at the Dean's office if she could give me information on a student off the computer. The office was in a huge wooden mansion which somebody had used as a house two hundred years ago. Now it was being used for the administration. The Dean's office was on the top floor, up red, wooden stairs. I told the secretary I was suspicious about a student's behavior.

'We're not allowed to give out personal information,' she told me. She was an overweight, older lady wearing a large, green dress.

'You're not?' I said.

'No.'

'But I'm security,' I said, trying to keep the plead out of my voice.

'Well, OK,' she said hesitantly. She glanced at me sourly like I was ruining her smooth day and looked down at her computer. 'What's the name?'

'Helen. I'm not sure of the last name.'

The secretary looked up. 'We can't do *any*thing without a last name.'

'Can't you just look up all the Helens? There can't be too many of them.'

'No,' she said and looked at me as if I was the suspicious one.

I walked out. I realized afterwards that was a pretty risky thing to do. I had to be more careful. One slip could ruin everything.

I had to find some other way to learn more about Helen. I had to do what I had wanted to avoid. I had to follow her. I couldn't think of any other way.

I waited, parked by the steps of the library to catch her on her way to class. From the place where I was parked I could see most of the heart of the campus. So not only didn't it seem like I was looking for somebody, it seemed like I was doing my job.

Students and professors walked by me. Some glanced at me. Most didn't. They all looked like they had a purpose. I had a purpose of my own. After about a half hour I saw her. I got out of the car, closed the door and locked it. I walked in her direction but never looked her way, I only kept her in my peripheral. She walked up a stone path leading to the classrooms on the edge of the campus. The path also led to the security office. I walked ten steps behind her. There was no way for anyone to know I was following her. She went inside a large white building which looked like a house, the oldest building on campus. I followed her inside. Just as I entered, I saw her go into room 110. I walked up to the door and opened it. There were only four students in the room, including Helen. The professor was sitting at the front of a big round table scratching his stomach.

'Is this—' I started to ask but my mind went blank. I was so intent on finding Helen, I hadn't thought of anything to say. 'History 101,' I finally said. I realized that was the dumbest class I could have chosen but I kept on looking at the professor with a hard grin.

'No,' the professor said seriously. 'This is Politics of Society.'

'Oh, I'm sorry,' I said.

As I walked out, I glanced at her. She was looking at me and smiling a little bit. I had never seen her that close before, without her face concealed behind the hood of her sweatshirt. Her face was smooth and olive-colored. She had a small head and wide eyes. Half her head seemed to be those wide eyes. I left the room with the vision of those eyes on the back of my own.

I asked the Student Affairs office for a list of students in Politics of Society at 2.30 on Tuesdays. The student working the desk didn't question me. He was an eager kid with damp black hair wearing a college sweatshirt. He began typing on a computer.

I was starting to enjoy this detective game.

'Would you like a printout?' he asked.

'Yes,' I said and looked around.

He handed it to me. I quickly looked the names over as I stood there. There was only one Helen on the list. Helen Childs.

I smiled slyly to myself. I had won.

I wanted to make the letter short and harmless. I struggled with four or five drafts before finally getting it right and stuffing it into a white, letter-sized envelope.

I knew that the head of security and administration would frown on me for sending her even a harmless letter like the one I'd written. But they didn't understand. They wanted to keep security and students apart. They didn't know that I was helping Helen more than I could help her with my nightstick and my keys.

As security, I had access to every post-office box in the mailroom. The last row of mailboxes was reserved for when there was over-enrollment. I used one of these boxes as my return address. The students who worked the mailroom wouldn't know the difference. And the box couldn't be traced to anybody.

I dropped the envelope with just the words 'Helen Childs' written on the front in ballpoint ink in the campus mail slot. Then I went back to work and waited. I patrolled in the red station wagon, driving around the campus four times, trying to think about something else, but I couldn't stop thinking about the letter. I wasn't sure if the letter I wrote was too forward, or not forward enough.

You don't know me. I've seen you around campus and I'd like to meet you but I don't know how to go about doing it. I'm shy in my own way. The reason I'm writing this is because I think we have something in common. We both want something out of life and we can't find it here. I thought we could meet

sometime. Help each other out. Save ourselves. Write back to
me at box 917.

I had another version which was more like a love letter. But I
didn't think that would work. The reason I liked her was because
she didn't go for the sap.

At that point there was nothing to do but wait and go on with
my job. I actually started doing the job pretty responsibly to keep
my mind off Helen and the letter. I'd give her a week to respond. I
was confident she would. Like I had said in the letter, she needed
saving, just like me.

Chapter Six

LAMBS WITH WOOL
SWEATERS

FOUR DAYS WENT by and there was nothing. But I felt fine
about it. She just needed some time to think it over. It wasn't
an easy thing to make changes in your life. I couldn't rush it.

In the meantime, I was more content than ever. I was almost
sure she'd write me back and then we could be together. I came
home at night and I didn't even need the TV. I'd sit in silence
and watch the wall, happy. A few times I caught my reflection in
the mirror and found that I had a big, bright smile I didn't realize
I had. The drawback was that I couldn't sleep much. I took to
drinking before I went to bed just to settle me down. About 6.00
one night I was fixing myself a whiskey and lemon iced tea just
to see what it tasted like when there was a knock on the door.

'Messenger,' said someone from behind the door.

I opened the door. A young guy with acne scars wearing a
suit stood at the door holding a package.

'Are you David?' he said.

'No. He lives one floor up.'

'Sorry. See, they just gave me the apartment building and not
the number of the apartment.'

'What is it?'

'What?'

'What's in the package.'

'Screenplay,' he said.

'David's a writer,' I said.

'I know. This is his screenplay.'

'Oh yeah?'

'I gotta go though, really,' he said and I watched him go up the stairs.

'First one on the right, I think,' I shouted after him. 'It's not the one right above me.'

He didn't answer.

David was one of the nicer people who lived above me in the building. He was somber with dark eyes and he looked like a tortured soul. He didn't live right above me. Two lesbians lived directly above me. Their bedroom was above mine but I never heard their bed creak. I'd never talked to either of them. One of them was real butch, silent, always with a belligerent frown. She wore football jerseys. The other looked like she could have been some businessman's wife. She was very feminine and only wore dresses. But she was a real man hater, I knew. She'd always give me strange, hateful smiles. It's ironic who lived next door to them. A guy of about medium build, short, dark, parted hair, and a big womanizer. I'd never seen him with the same girl twice. He was average looking, but not ugly. Age would probably hit him like a fist. I guessed he was meeting as many women as he could while he still looked his best. The lesbians must have always been hearing sex pounding through the walls.

The writer named David lived next to him. Those were the only people I knew on the first floor. I think the rest were old people. It was a big place, you see, I couldn't know everybody. On the second floor I knew a woman named Daisy. I talked to her occasionally and I liked her fine. Her name really was Daisy, it wasn't a nickname. But she wasn't as pretty as her name. She was thin up top, wide in the hips and had gone prematurely gray. She was a housewife. Sometimes I thought about her but she was married. Her husband's name was Joe and he fit his name, the kind of guy who would pump gas. He ran some stores that sold something, I didn't know what.

Those were the only people I'd met. Meeting people wasn't easy. I saw a lot of tenants walking in and out of the building but

I never talked to them. I didn't want to go through the trouble. If they wanted to meet me I'd be happy to talk to them but I wasn't about to go knocking on doors.

I was leaving my apartment to go to the liquor store to get some more whiskey – the iced tea drink was good – when I saw David. He was young and lean, underfed but good looking.

'Did you get your screenplay?' I asked.

'What?'

'Your screenplay.'

'Yeah, I did, how—'

'The guy came to my apartment by mistake.'

'Oh. Sorry. They gave it back to me with all these rewrite notes that don't make any sense.' He looked bothered, pre-occupied.

'What's it about?'

'It would take too long to go into it.'

'Well, basically.'

'Basically, it's about divorce.'

'Like *Kramer vs. Kramer*,' I said happily.

He cringed. 'Yeah. Like *Kramer vs. Kramer*.'

'I've lived in this city long enough to get to know about these things.'

He didn't say anything.

'So you're trying to make it in the movie business? It must be hard.'

He obviously wanted to go but I couldn't stop myself from talking to him. I needed to show him I was decent. 'It's a cut-throat business, huh?'

'Yes,' he said to the ground.

He took a step away from me as if to leave.

'I've thought about writing a screenplay myself,' I said. 'Doesn't seem too hard. It's an easy way to get involved. I have lots of ideas. Murder plots, assassination dramas. There's a great one about a president with three heads, all with different party affiliations. I don't have a title but that seems like a pretty good start. I thought about *President Waffle*. I'll tell you about them one of these days.'

'Sure,' he said. 'I've got to go now.' He mumbled, 'Meeting,' and quickly walked away.

I was frozen still. Shit, if I'm the one to run away from, David. I thought the three-head idea was pretty good. I made it up on the spot. I had never thought of it before in my life. So don't treat me like an unwanted stranger. I'm not the person who comes up on the street and begs for money. I'm not the annoying guy at the party who asks you what's your favorite color. I'm not the lunatic. I'm on the good side. If this life is about good versus evil, I am definitely on the good side.

When Helen didn't reply to my first letter I decided to write her a second, just to let her know I was serious. This time there was more of a sureness in the way I wrote the letter. Last time I thought maybe I was too weak. I sounded like she should only write me back if she felt like it. Obviously I didn't give her enough incentive to write me back.

> *Hello. It's me again. I was serious when I wrote you last time. I thought maybe you didn't take me seriously. I think we should get together. It's not only that I think we should see each other, but that we must see each other. For our health. I think we are both unhappy here, wondering if there's something more. There has got to be something deeper to life. Your friends don't know anything about us, about real people, about thinkers. They hide behind all their socializing and their money. There is nothing real about them. You and I are like-minded people. We have been let down many times in our lives. What better people can get along? I am a good person. I want to help. I like you. I am here for you. It could be good for both our lives.*

I signed the letter, 'Someone who cares.'

This time I was going to go about sending the letter differently. I wanted to watch her open the letter so I could really see how she felt.

I put the letter in the mailbox and waited. I sat in the car across from the mailroom and stared at the door. The time was 2.00. Nobody came by to see where I was. I got a few calls on the radio, one to help a professor move some files from one office to another, another about some lost keys, but eventually somebody else dealt with it. At 3.30 she still wasn't there. I knew she wasn't in class. Where could she be? I was restless. I got out of the car and went to the mailroom to see if the letter had been distributed. I opened the door and it shut with a slam. Fred, the head postal worker, said hello with a smile. He was thin, freckled and usually smiling.

'What you in here for, Ray?' he said.

'I sent something to a . . . professor and I wanted to see if it got to him. I need him to get it today.'

'We're doing it right now. He'll get it. What's his name?'

'OK, thanks,' I said and walked out.

When I was halfway to my car I saw Helen walking to the mailroom. I went quickly to the car, got in, locked the door, and sat down. I started shivering. I opened the window for some air. I thought maybe I was getting fever-cold.

I sat there for ten minutes. She must have been talking to friends. Twelve minutes exactly, she came out. I could see my letter tucked against her notebook under her arm. I waited a few moments until she was almost out of sight. I got out of the car and followed her. Luckily she didn't walk too far before she sat down to open her mail. She sat down on a sawed-off tree trunk set along the walkway. I couldn't find a place to stand without seeming like I was looking at her. To my left there was a classroom with a window and a class was in session. Some bored students' wandering eyes were looking my way. I looked to my right. There was a staircase leading up to a building. In the door to the building there was a small glass porthole window. I ran up the stairs and tried the door. It was locked. I opened it with my skeleton key.

I stood behind the door and watched. Behind me was deserted, a cold hallway that led to the back of the cafeteria kitchen.

Helen hadn't opened my letter yet. It still lay on her thighs, her knees locked together. She was looking at the school's weekly newsletter, no expression at all on her face. My letter was right below. She set the newsletter aside. She picked up my letter, that familiar white envelope, and stared at it. She opened the envelope, a little anxiously I thought, like maybe she was eager. She peered inside, maybe to see if there was anything more than a letter in there. Then she took the letter out and began to read. She didn't move a muscle. Halfway through she stopped reading and slowly looked from left to right. I didn't flinch. She finished reading and put the letter back, slowly and carefully, as if she didn't want to crease it. A good sign. I couldn't gauge her expression. She didn't look angry or upset. And she didn't throw the letter away. She tucked it right back under the newsletter and sat on the stump, staring ahead of her. She didn't look upset, but she didn't look happy either. Although in the time I'd known her I'd never seen her very happy. That's what I liked about her. Sitting on the stump, she was just thinking. Maybe she was thinking of a way to write me back. She looked kind of content sitting on that stump, not nervous or restless, but like she'd come into some peaceful news. Soon she got up and walked away.

I walked back to the car. Bud was saying over the CB, 'Ray? Are you there?'

I picked up. 'Hello,' I said.

'Where the hell have you been?' he said.

'I went to the bathroom.'

'Oh. Well, do you know anything about some keys a student left in our office?'

I said I didn't.

'All right,' he said and shut off.

I sat in the car and took ten deep breaths and tried to stop the shaking.

Two days went by and there was no reply. I was getting anxious. I was also getting resentful. But I went along with my job as usual. Somebody else helped that professor move his files and dropped them. They spilled all over the cement path, mixing all of the files together. They lay in disorder. The professor came to the office and yelled at me about it. I told him sorry. He stared at me bitterly like I was a spoiled infant. Besides that, everything was normal. The job was becoming as routine as the warehouse.

Then I saw something I wished I never had. Walking through campus from lunch, I saw Helen talking, hands locked, with another guy. I was drinking a hot cup of coffee when I saw them. The coffee burned, but when I saw them I drank it down fast and didn't even feel it. The guy was only a little taller than her, wearing dark blue pants and a flannel shirt. He had just enough stubble to fake a goatee. I hadn't ever seen him before. They looked serious together. Stern faces, as if this was business. Maybe they even looked conceited, as if nothing existed but them. I watched them for ten minutes. They just sat there, talking. He rubbed her hand and she smiled. Helen gave a slight glance my way as if she knew I was there. She looked over with an I-don't-care-about-you expression and then nuzzled close to him. I had the feeling that she knew it was me who was writing the letters. Why else would she have looked over like that? She was ignoring me on purpose. And she was parading her new boyfriend in front of the world.

I got up and watched them move to the lawn in front of the administration mansion. She lightly kissed him, eyes closed. He was sitting cross-legged, she was leaning against him. He looked thin and weak, almost as if he couldn't support her weight. She was wearing that same damn sweatshirt. She brushed some grass off her legs, then she kissed him again. He said something to her. She nodded.

I could tell right away that he was nobody. She was settling for something less than her, like she had with her other friends. After all my letters, she was ignoring me, choosing someone beneath her. Or maybe she was nothing at all either. Maybe she was just like her friends. Maybe I had been fooled.

I went back to the security office, sat in a back room where nobody could see me and began writing a third letter. Unlike the other letters, I wrote this one by hand. I wrote it in one draft without stopping, the pen pressed hard to the page.

I saw you with that boyfriend of yours. Who is he? Does he care about you? Not like me. I would care for you like you've never been cared for before. I know the pains of the world so I know how to avoid them. I could have been your shelter. But you ignored me. If only you knew what you were ignoring. One day I'm going to be great and you'll regret you ever let me go. I'm the one. Do you have so much better to do? I've seen your friends. They're not very interesting, like most people here. They care only about themselves. And what do they care about? Frail, vile, boring people like themselves. Maybe like you. Do you want to be like that? The more you stay with them, the more you sink into their mold. I thought you wanted to get away. I was wrong. You're just as weak. You don't even deserve my time. You're just as selfish because you won't even write me back. But remember, I've got the upper hand. I know who you are but you don't know me. I'm the one and you didn't realize it. You're too petty. Maybe the best way to get back is to get revenge.

The longer I wrote, the angrier I got. I couldn't help it. I meant the things I said. This place wasn't any good for her, I could tell. She was rejecting me for ugliness. And there was already so much ugliness, so vile, like her friends. She didn't even deserve my time.

If she couldn't love me at least she could fear me. I was a good man, strong with the power of words and conviction. I was the one who knew the loss of the world. I was the one with insight. I wasn't the one who was worthless, she was. If she couldn't see that, she deserved a small token of my bitter esteem.

I walked back to the grass quad where they were sitting. They were still there, holding each other. Helen's dorm, Sheffield, was just on the other side of the quad. I had found out where she lived from some files in the security office. I walked toward Sheffield. She lived in room 316. I walked up the cold stairs to the third floor. The hallway had a thin orange carpet. Each door was brown with a metal doorknob. The students had put up various adolescent things on the doors, mostly pictures cut out from magazines. I was at 316. Helen's door was empty. I looked left then right. No one was in the hallway so I opened the door with my skeleton key and walked in.

The room was small, just a bed, a desk, and a closet attached to a dresser under a square mirror. There were papers all over the desk and a few books on the shelf above. Most of the stuff was on the floor, clothes, books, make-up. The room smelled strongly of dirty clothes. But it didn't smell bad. A girl's dirt never smelled as bad. The windows were closed and the air was thick. I smelled Helen's sweet, damp smell.

One thing I noticed was a book called *The Joy of Teasing*, but I didn't have time to pick it up. There were two other books – *Marx for Beginners* and a sociology textbook. I looked around for a place to put the letter. Her bed was unmade, with orange sheets. I went to the bed and set the letter down by the pillow. When I looked closely at the orange sheets, the color of a pumpkin, I saw that the sheets were stained. The stains were round, almost clear, with a dark edge. I imagined Helen and her boyfriend having sex among all the dirty clothes and books on the floor.

I thought I heard shuffling in the hallway. I realized that I might have been taking too long. Right before I was about to leave, I took the letter off the bed. If they knew someone got into the room, they would figure that the person who left the letter had access. They could come around and pin it on me. Instead, I lay the letter on the floor by the door, as if I had slipped it under the doorway.

I had seen enough. I had seen her room. I had seen those stains. I knew what I was up against.

The next day when I walked into the security office Bud said to me, 'We've got a problem.'

'What is it?'

'Come here,' he said. He brought me to a table in the back. My letters were there. The envelopes were stacked on the side. He stared at me gravely. For a long second I thought I was caught. But he said, 'A girl came in and complained about a guy harassing her.'

'Really.'

'You should see the letters he wrote. Awful things. Just read this—'

'I don't think I want to.'

He looked sad. 'Yeah, you're better off. She was shook up about it. She even started to cry.'

My first instinct was regret. But then that changed. Then I felt nothing at all.

'This is serious, now. Something like this has never happened here. We're gonna have to crack down. Things are going to have to change. I want to catch this guy. Sick fuck.'

I'd never heard Bud swear before.

His flustered anger made me smile.

I felt good then. I was changing the course of things. I was changing policy. I'd shocked them into action.

'Any idea who it is?' I asked.

'He left a box number, but that's an empty box. It's not assigned to anyone.'

'Smart guy.'

'Not that smart. We'll find him. My guess is that once he finds out we're involved, he'll slow down.'

Bud was more right than he knew. I had to quit the job. I probably had to quit right away. I didn't want to be involved once there were other people looking for me. I'd go after people, sure, but what's the fun in being followed?

Chapter Seven

THE ICE-CREAM TRUCKS

THE NEXT DAY, bad timing, I got a call from my mom. My mother and father had gotten a divorce five years earlier. Throughout my childhood they hadn't really gotten along. They treated their marriage like a no parole sentence. When I was twenty-two, they realized they would end up killing each other so they decided to end it. I wasn't against the divorce. After my tenth birthday, when my mother threw my birthday cake at my dad after he called it 'pasty,' our family never got along anyway.

What I did mind was seeing her go out with guy after guy, sometimes my age. She was in her late forties, I didn't know her actual age, but she dated like she was in high school. She had these breasts, you see.

My dad was old and alone. He had a kitchen pantry full of cans of vegetable soup and frozen food. Sometimes he got prostitutes. He told me I should do the same.

They both lived within three blocks of each other in Silverlake. The gangs were creeping closer and closer to their front yards. My mom lived in the house where I grew up, small but nice, and when I was a kid those streets were safe and quiet, the only noise coming from married couples inside the houses.

My childhood was all right, for the most part. I won't go that deeply into it. It was filled with the usual amount of harassment, nothing too serious, but nothing too easy either. Their recent divorce hit me hard at first but then I realized after a couple of months that I didn't care. I rarely saw them after I left home anyway.

My mother still dressed like a prim little housewife, bright colors but controlled, and she still talked in that condescending mother tone. But she dated feverishly, partly to prove something to my father, but also to prove something to herself, sow the wild oats she hadn't done when she married out of high school.

Her voice was coarse from cigarettes and all the different guys' tongues she'd taken down her throat.

Somehow, through all that, she still talked like a mother.

'Are you working?' she asked.

'I have a job as a security guard.'

'Oh really?' she asked with some pride.

'Yeah.'

'What happened to the warehouse?'

'I quit.'

'Oh. Why?'

'So I could get a job as a security guard.'

'Oh.'

There was a silence.

'Why are you calling me?' I asked.

'Can't I call my son?'

'I'm your son?'

'C'mon, Ray.' I hated the way she said my name. She put extra emphasis on the Y, as if my name was Freddy or Henry. Ray-y, she said. She gave me the name and she couldn't even pronounce it.

'Are you dating anyone?' she asked.

'No, are you?'

'Now c'mon, Ray-y. I want to *learn* something about you. We haven't talked in months.'

'I would have called, but . . .' I stopped.

'But what?'

'But I don't like you very much.'

'Now, Ray-y, why do you have to be so difficult?'

'It's in my genes. I inherited it.'

'From who?' I could hear her smiling.

'I don't want to play this game.'

'Well, OK. I just wanted to hear how you were doing.'

'I'm doing fine.'

'OK.'

'OK.'

'Bye.'

'Right.'

We hung up. All our phone calls were the same. I wondered if phone calls all over the place went the same way. They probably did.

I called up my father. I got his answering machine. 'This is Jerry Tompkins. Leave a message and I'll get back to you.' Beep. Bored and sad-voiced. 'Mom's dating someone younger than me,' I said and hung up.

I quit working at the college. When I quit, Bud said, 'But why?' as if he couldn't understand why anybody would quit such a fine job. The withered man thinking, I've spent twenty-five wonderful years here. He looked at me like he was losing a son. I told him I needed to move on. There were important things for me to do beyond the college walls. He didn't suspect anything about Helen. He liked the job too much to ever suspect an employee.

I missed Helen. I couldn't help thinking about her after I left. Although it wasn't really her I was thinking about. I had resigned myself to the fact that she wasn't right. She was already tainted. What I missed more than Helen was the search. I'd still picture her smooth, unsmiling face, the way she didn't lift up her feet when she walked, her gray sweatshirt. But when I pictured her I also pictured myself slowly walking after her, deceitful but inconspicuous, breaking into her room, smelling her strong, unfamiliar scent, and having no one know that I was the one sending the letters. Even thinking about it gave me a rush of adrenaline hope. But now all that was gone.

I tried writing her a fourth letter, but nothing came out. I was forcing it. There was no fear in being caught. I thought about asking for the job back, but if I continued with Helen and got caught I'd be in more trouble than I wanted.

So Helen was gone. I was back to where I was before. I was dead-tired angry. I was no one. I could sit watching TV for weeks and it wouldn't matter. No one would notice. If I didn't leave the apartment for weeks no one would call the police or even blink an eye. I had enough money to stay at home. What I didn't have was anyone but myself. The person I really liked was Marta. But she was gone too. Goddamn Marta. I really did like her. But now I was nothing. How could she like me if I was nothing? I couldn't compare to industry Bill. I didn't have a job. I probably didn't even have her as a friend anymore. And what's more, the ice-cream trucks were back.

Those trucks could drive a man mad. The apartment I lived in before this one was also plagued by the same trucks. The trucks played the same song, only about ten notes long, over and over and over. And of course these trucks only came around in summer when I had to leave the windows open so the song would pour through my apartment. The truck drove around my neighborhood maybe ten hours a day. Even when it was far away I could still hear it, the memory of that little song stuck in my head. *Da Da D/Da D/Da D/Da, Da Da D/Da D/Da Da*. Long after the truck was gone I would have that song running through my head while I was trying to sleep.

Those trucks followed me, I believed it. They were a symptom of something worse, something much larger. Maybe I had something better in store for myself. Maybe I was just paying my dues. And maybe part of paying my dues was going a little crazy.

For now the best thing I could do for myself was watch TV.

Let me tell you about me and the TV. Some might say I was justifying myself to you. Apologizing a little. That's not the case. As a kid I was shy and reserved, apologizing for the pimples on my face. Now I had grown out of acne and that kind of thinking. And, I'll tell you, even if I was apologizing for watching TV, that wouldn't matter much. Apology accepted. All you can do is sit back and listen.

I'm just stating where I stand. The TV was a good method of therapy. A friend when no one's home.

I watched TV for two solid weeks, catching up on daytime TV. I even followed a couple of the stories on *The Young and the Restless* for three days straight, but then I gave it up. I watched the talk shows instead. They started at seven o'clock in the morning and didn't stop until the local news at five. I watched most of them. All about failed marriages, failed relationships, men are pigs, women with eating disorders, ways to decorate your home, satanic cults, people who are disfigured, overweight people, new fall fashions, people who decorate themselves with metal and paint, celebrities, a man who slept with both the mother and her daughter and got them both pregnant, crazy people, racism, sexism, militia members, the absence of a work ethic, molested children, gangs, interviews with celebrity inmates, the inner cities, and the gun problem.

Chapter Eight

THE BOTTOM OF THINGS

I WAS EATING at a restaurant called Patrick's Roadhouse, a place by the beach with lime-green walls and run by people from the past, when the unexpected happened. A woman came up and started talking to me. I don't know why this happened, it just did. I looked bad, unshaven, wearing shades of brown, and had that bored look of the unemployed. I was eating a BLT with ripe avocado. The woman looked something like Marta. Though I didn't like doing that. I compared all women I saw to Marta because she was the only woman I'd really known in the past five years. This woman, she said her name was Joyce, a regular name, came up and sat at my table. On any other day it would have been a fantasy, but on this day I didn't feel like talking to anyone. I was alone and thinking about television and murder.

Joyce was I guessed about thirty-five. She was the same height as me and under her aged skin I could see real beauty. But she was dressed cheap and without care so she looked like she didn't want to be approached herself.

She sat down at my table and said, 'May I?' and took a fry off my plate.

'Why does this happen?' I asked her.

'What happen?'

'I haven't met anyone for the last five years and here you sit down.'

She gave a little smile. But I was actually annoyed. Sometimes things were easy, but most times they weren't, and that's what bothered me.

'I don't know,' she said. 'You don't look so approachable.'

That was insulting. Who was she to tell me how I looked? She was a stranger. I didn't say anything and ate the rest of my fries before she could eat any more of them.

'What's your name?' she asked.

'Ray,' I said and continued eating. I wasn't playing it aloof, I really didn't want to be talking to her. I had other things on my mind.

We sat in silence.

'Not too talkative,' she said.

'Who? You or me?'

'You.'

'Well, you're the one who sat down. Don't you have something you want to talk about?'

'Hey, most men would be proud to have me sit down at their table.'

I smiled. I liked that. She was dead serious.

'So what did you sit down here for?' I said.

'I wanted to talk to you.'

'Why?'

'I liked the way you look.'

'You just said I didn't look approachable.'

'That's what I liked.'

'There's a lot of guys who don't look approachable. Homeless guys don't look approachable.'

'Right,' she said and had an angrier reaction than I had intended. She got up to leave. I didn't make a motion for her to stay. She walked to the back of the restaurant, turned around and came back.

'Don't you want me to stay?' she asked pleadingly.

'It doesn't matter to me.'

'Wouldn't you right now like to have me on my back? I have a good body under here.' She pointed to her loose-fitting, half-polyester clothes. 'Isn't that what you're thinking about?'

'Don't flatter yourself.'

At this point I was enjoying myself. Believe it or not, she was real easy to talk to. And she had a pathetic kind of sadness to her that I understood. When I tried talking to most women I clammed up and couldn't utter a word. With her, I was coming back with answers like they were scripted. And yeah, I did try to imagine those polyester clothes off of her and it was a decent sight.

'Come with me,' she said, grabbing my arm, and she pulled me out of the restaurant. I wasn't completely done with my sandwich. It wasn't until we were three blocks away that I realized I hadn't paid for my meal. I told her I wanted to go back. 'Don't worry,' she said. 'They won't know the difference.' This bothered me because I liked Patrick's and ate there often. She walked on, guiltless.

She walked me to her apartment, not far from mine. It was a small place, a studio, with a living room big enough for a couch and TV and a bedroom big enough for a bed and a table. The kitchen was as narrow as a stove. In comparison, my trailer-park apartment looked big. In the living room there was only one thing on the dirty white walls, a small framed poster for a movie called *Diana's Heat*. The picture was of a woman bent over with her hands on her knees, smiling prettily. In the background was a poster for another movie, this time the same woman standing between two men, one in a suit and one wearing only shorts, with the title in bold red letters, *Blonde on Blonde*.

'Is that you?' I asked.

She was sitting on the edge of the couch with a confused look like she didn't know if she should sit or stand.

'That's me. I'm Diana.'

'I thought your name was Joyce.'

'Diana's my *thea*ter name.'

'What's wrong with Joyce?'

'I wanted to use the name Diana. I've never liked the name Joyce.'

'Joyce is a fine name. Never be ashamed of your name.'

She stared at me, wide-eyed. Then she sank back into the couch.

'So, ah, is that porn?' I asked.

'Well, have you ever seen porn?'

I got quick flashes of pretty, naked women made ugly by video light.

'What?' I said.

'Have you ever seen a porn film?'

'Yes.'

'The movies I did are nothing like the films they have now. There was much more care put into the films I made. They had plots and dialogues, and back then we used real film.'

She said all this with a strange degree of pride. She stared at the poster with a glazed look. She was crazy. I wanted to get out of there.

But I also wanted to keep her sad look company.

'Do you want to see one of them?' she asked and made a move for the TV shelf.

'Are you serious?'

'Yes,' she said.

'Watch you have sex with other men?'

'Yes.'

'I don't think that would be right.'

'They're not all about sex, you know,' she said, annoyed. 'Some of them are beautiful. In *Blonde on Blonde* we filmed on a deserted beach a little past Malibu. There was an abandoned pier. The weather was so perfect that day.'

She looked into the air wistfully.

'I really don't want to see it,' I said. I didn't. At least not with her sitting there.

'You sure?'

'Yes.'

'OK,' she conceded. She cowered back to the couch, disappointed.

'No one wants to see my old films anymore,' she said sadly, like a hurt girl, not looking at me.

I was about to say I'd like to see one just to make her feel better, wipe that expression away, when she said, 'Excuse me,' and went to the bathroom, a small closet even smaller than mine. I sat and thought about all this for a while. Here I was sitting in an aging porn actress's apartment. She came back and sat on the couch next to me. Our legs were five feet apart but our feet were touching.

'I don't do them anymore,' she said, breaking a silence.

'No, I'd think not.'

'What's that mean?' she said angrily.

'What I mean is that you're . . . older than most of them now.'

For some reason this appeased her. She sank back down into the couch. 'I'm happy,' she said, almost a question.

It was like none of this was really happening. I didn't even have dreams like this, meeting an old porn star and sitting in her dark apartment. That was why when she started to take her clothes off, I said, 'No.' There was something very wrong going on in that apartment. Things that didn't happen in dreams shouldn't happen in real life. And she was acting strange now. Once we got to her apartment, she no longer led me around, but looked as if she didn't know where she was. She looked lost. Her sadness was beyond even my own. Sex with her was tempting but it was wrong.

Marta had done some stripping when she was younger and when she talked about it she looked the same way as Joyce sitting here now.

'I've met plenty of strippers but I've never met a porn actress before,' I said as she pulled her shirt back down to her waist.

She looked at me icily. 'There's nothing wrong with that.'

'No, I didn't—'

'Everyone's got something in their past. Don't you? Don't you have something in your past that other people would frown on? Everybody's got something to hide.'

I liked her right there. I didn't answer. She answered for me.

'Sure you do. Sure you do. Everybody does.'

I did. And she knew just by looking at me. The old porn star and the ex-security guard had something in common.

'What do you do now?' I asked.

'I work for an escort service,' she said. Then she clarified, 'For older women.'

She smiled, teeth the color of newspaper. After all the weird looks and strange talk, this was her idea of a joke.

She stopped her smile. 'You know sex films aren't that different from other movies.'

'No?'

'No. Just as many people see them and a lot of work goes into getting them done. Some of them are very pretty and stylized. Some Hollywood directors got their start in porn. Did you know that?'

'No.'

'It's true.'

'Why are you telling me this?' I thought out loud.

'I thought you were interested.'

'Not really. Let's talk about something else.'

'OK. What?'

'You choose.'

'Well, my friend's having a party tonight. Do you wanna come?'

'Sure,' I said. I grabbed for a walnut sitting on a table in a blue dish. But then I saw there wasn't a nutcracker.

'There's only one thing,' she said.

'What's that?'

'It's a cast party.'

Chapter Nine

HOMELESS PROM NIGHT

OUT OF DEPRESSION and into the gutter. Joyce's gutter was filled with sometimes-smiling, tan, sex-driven faces.

She kept telling me on the way to the party not to worry, 'These people are just like you and me.' I wasn't very much like Joyce so I was worried.

'What's this a cast party for?' I asked.

'A movie,' she said.

'Which movie?'

'*Risqué Business.*'

'Yeah?'

'You know, like that movie, *Risky Business?*'

'Got that.'

I looked at Joyce as we drove there in her small, brown Toyota. It was the same model as my car, same year, which I thought was strange and a bad omen. Joyce kind of looked like a homeless person out on the town. She had on too much make-up, shades of blue. And she was wearing a short black skirt, wide in her hips, but which showed off long, thin legs which were scratched and in some places scarred.

'Have you seen the movie?' I asked her.

'No, but I've seen others that they've done. Cherry Blossom is the real star. She'll be there. You'll get to meet her.'

Most times I got nervous when I went to parties. My stomach would shake and I'd even get gas. But on the way to this party I wasn't. Joyce was as relaxed as putty and so lacked in cynicism that it seemed like none of this was happening.

'You'll like Cherry,' she said.

'Now, tell me again, why did you invite me to this and not somebody else?'

I'd been asking her this in moments of silence.

'Like I said, I liked the way you look. You look how I feel. Used.'

'I guess I feel that way too.'

'Yeah?'

'Yeah.'

'Used.'

'Hmmn.'

She smiled at me with her grim, pale-gray teeth. While she was still looking at me, she put her foot on the brake and pulled the car to a stop. 'We're here,' she said.

We were in West Hollywood. The apartment was like any other in LA – three stories high, white with some brown trim, built in the last twenty or thirty years. When you went inside it seemed unsolid and hollow.

We took the linoleum elevator to the fourth floor and knocked on a plain, gray door.

A man with bleached-blond hair wearing a tank-top and short shorts showing off long, bronze skin opened the door.

'Ken,' Joyce said happily.

'Hi, Joyce. Glad you could,' he paused and looked at me, 'make it.'

'Your name really Ken?' I asked him as we walked inside, which was meant to be a joke but which came out as an insult.

'Like the doll,' he said seriously and looked at Joyce.

'Sorry,' I told Joyce as we walked in.

'It's fine. Everything's fine,' she said, her eyes toward the ceiling.

She walked into the front room looking up and around her, like a little girl coming to Disneyland.

Inside, people were mingling like at any party, holding a glass of wine or beer nervously in front of their faces. Most of the people were much more tan than normal, and some leathery dark like Joyce, so the floor of the living room appeared to be a sea of bare, golden flesh.

The apartment itself was small and sparse. There was only a couch in the living room and bare, white stucco walls, like the occupants had just moved into the apartment. It wasn't a very good place for a party, really. People were stuck up against each other like cattle riding in a semi-truck.

I walked in, my hand on Joyce's back, as she led the way.

'Here, come with me,' she said.

We headed straight for the kitchen and got beers out of a refrigerator packed with five different kinds of beer, imported and domestic.

She led me to a corner of the living room. Here, there, people said, 'Hi, Joyce,' and gave me a short glance, sizing me up.

'Who do you want to meet first?' she said.

'How should I know? I don't know any of these people.'

But the problem was solved. A man and woman walked up to us. They looked alike so I figured they were married. They had the same beak-like nose and curly brown hair. Though they looked as if maybe they were in the middle of a divorce because they both stared out from stolid, bitter faces.

'Hello, Joyce,' they said together in monotone.

'Hi,' Joyce said back with party cheer. She looked at me. 'I'd like you to meet Bob and Fishy Taylor.'

'Fishy?'

'Yes.'

'Everyone's got a weird name around here.'

'I got the name in elementary school when the boys used to look up my skirt and say it smelled like fish. They gave me the nickname Fishy.'

Joyce giggled. 'I love that story,' she said.

Bob grunted like he'd heard this story too many times.

I'd heard the story once and that was too many times.

'How are you guys?' Joyce asked.

'We're getting divorced,' said Fishy.

'Oh, that's terrible,' Joyce said with genuine sadness and began rubbing Fishy's cashmere shoulder.

'Yes,' said Fishy.

They turned and left us. They'd given the information and now they were moving on.

'That's terrible about them,' Joyce told me. 'They were some of the first people I knew who married. They did all their films together.'

'Oh, really.'

We stood there for a while but nobody came up to talk to us. After some time, Joyce said, 'I want you to meet Cherry Blossom. She's my favorite.'

We walked through the nest of people to the bedroom. The bedroom was empty except for an old green chair, a double bed with nothing on it but a white sheet, and two people sitting on the maroon-carpeted floor.

'Here she is,' Joyce said.

Joyce grabbed my hand and took me over to the seated people, a man and a woman. The guy had a thick mustache and blondish hair, orange as if dyed. He was wearing too-tight black pants and a yellow-collared shirt with the lizard sign. She was wearing a red leather mini-skirt and a white tank-top. From behind I could see a sliver of skin between the shirt and her skirt.

Joyce tapped the woman's shoulder. When she turned around I saw that she was just a girl, young and unblemished. She was another Helen. Some women, some people in general, had a certain glow. They usually only had it when they were younger, when they hadn't seen the sins of the world. Helen was slowly learning those sins and I saw that glow fading. This girl here had Helen's shy smile and the same dark color hair, but hers was short and thick with light streaks. She wasn't fake-tan like the other tanning salon bodies at the party. She was pure and sweet and real.

'This is Cherry Blossom,' Joyce said with almost motherly pride.

'Don't call me that,' the girl said. 'Just call me Sherry.'

'Sherry,' I stumbled out.

'This is Ray, Sherry. I met him at a restaurant.'

'That's great, Joyce. You're always telling me how you're not meeting people.'

Sherry smiled up at me. Joyce gave me a how-about-her grin.

'It's good to meet you,' I said. 'I'm Ray.'

Joyce and Sherry had a long, painful giggle.

'Sit down,' said Sherry.

As Joyce and I were sitting, the guy with the mustache said, 'I'm gonna go in the other room,' looking at me and Joyce with a real degree of snobbery, and left.

I sat down and just looked at Sherry. She was the most beautiful and pure girl I'd ever seen. Smooth-skinned and warm, as if radiating heat. And I didn't even have to sneak around to meet her. She was right here.

She asked, 'So what do you do, Ray?'

'I was a security guard for a while but I just quit.'

'Security?' She looked at Joyce seriously. 'I heard Frank was looking for security of some sort.' She looked back at me. 'I think he needs a bodyguard. He's getting so popular now, people recognize him on the street. I'm sure you could do the job. You look big and strong.'

My heart ached.

'So what do you do?' I asked.

'I'm an actress.'

'Really?'

'Mm-hmmn. I moved here from Minnesota a few years back and tried to make it in the movies. It's harder than you think.' She stopped and looked at me as if waiting for an answer.

'I imagine—'

'I ended up only being an extra in commercials,' she continued.

'Can you believe it? They said I had too plain a face. You have to be something really special, or else you're nothing.' She looked sad for a brief, brief moment but then said cheerfully, 'Hollywood's tough. It can be mean to some people. But I frown on all that now. It's better for me here. People are good to me. People like Joyce.' She gave Joyce a soft squeeze on the shoulder and ran her fingers through Joyce's bangs. 'She's been my idol for so long. Have you seen any of her films?'

'No.'

That's when I realized what Sherry meant when she said, 'actress.' Before I had time to think about it the guy with the mustache came back and said, 'It's time, Cherry,' and gave me a mean, dull look.

Joyce looked at me apologetically.

'What?' I said to her expression.

'You didn't really get to talk to Cherry.'

'That's fine.'

'She's my favorite.'

'Why?'

'Couldn't you see? She's just like I was. She's so, so . . .' She was too wistful to complete the sentence. 'Anyway, you'll get to see in a few minutes.' She pointed to the bed in the corner of the room.

I watched as Sherry walked to the bed. She was smooth and small, only about five foot two. She looked down at her arms as if to inspect them for damage. Then she took off her shirt. She didn't turn around. Her soft, coffee-tan back was to the room. Slowly, people began pouring into the room, all with a blank, zombie look in their eyes. Next, Sherry took off her mini-skirt. She was wearing a blue G-string. Then she took that off. I didn't know what to think. My mind was as blank as those zombie eyes, shocked into emptiness.

Sherry was standing by the bed looking down at herself, down at her thin waist, her evenly tan body, her shaved-straight line of public hair. Soon people were crowded around the bed. When the room was packed, the guy with the mustache walked into the room wearing different clothes than he had on before. He was wearing tight, black jeans, and a white T-shirt with a box of cigarettes tucked into the sleeve.

'That's Don Gold,' Joyce whispered to me.

Music came from somewhere, a slow, straight-from-porn instrumental.

The night's entertainment began. Sherry lay down on the bed like she was sleeping, curled up like a puppy. Don walked up to the bed and Sherry opened her eyes. She looked up at him like she was startled. Then she sat at the edge of the bed and started undoing his pants. As she pulled his limp dick out of his pants and it flopped into her hands, she looked up at him with sweet eyes. She began slowly and gently stroking his cock. She took it into her mouth and began slowly licking it, her soft, innocent lips falling over the head, her small left hand holding the base. I couldn't help but get a hard-on. Then she began doing it faster and faster. She started doing it so fast that it seemed like she didn't want to be doing it at all, moving her head so fast that everything was a blur, and she was no longer at the party, in front of people. So fast it was machine-like. Don Gold made quiet, unsentimental groans.

If you've ever seen porn, you know how the rest turns out. She sucks him off, he sucks her off, they suck off each other. Then he gets her on her back, then her stomach, ass to the air.

Everybody watching was sweating. The room was cramped with people. Some people were rubbing themselves. Some men had their hand up a woman's skirt, or vice versa. A woman was sucking off a guy in the corner, so jammed against the wall that she had to keep his dick deep in her throat. Joyce looked on with a wide, almost proud, smile. I was too horrified to be shocked. I had lost feeling. I watched everything no differently than if I was watching it on TV.

It was like watching Helen and her nobody boyfriend going at it, staining her dorm-room sheets. That made me angry. Watching

Sherry's small, bright face pressed to the bed, moaning, was like watching a new car getting crushed in the compactor, stripped of all life and grace.

She was on top of him, riding him as fast as a basketball being dribbled, one of his fingers sliding in and out of her ass. He must have said something to her because she quickly got off him and went back down on him, sucking him off as he came. She licked up and down, the cum spurting into her face and hair and she screamed, 'I want more cum.' She rubbed herself with one finger as if to keep herself interested.

Then it was over. People applauded. Somebody said, 'Encore,' and everybody laughed.

Don Gold lay on the bed on his back, wet with sweat. Sherry looked at the crowd, almost primly, cum all over her face and hair. She got up and walked into the other room. I heard the shower go on. Don put on his pants and began talking to another woman. People walked back into the living room and things resumed.

I couldn't stay in that room any longer. There was the strong smell of sweat and sex and the lingering hum of Sherry's final words.

'I need some air,' I told Joyce.

'OK,' she said.

We walked through the living room onto a small porch, just as cramped with bodies. But at least outside there was air and the smell of sex wasn't so thick. We weren't standing there thirty seconds before a man, large with hair coming out all sides of his shirt, took Joyce by the shoulders and said, 'Where were you?'

She didn't answer.

'Where were you?' he said again. 'Cunt.' He hung in front of Joyce like a dam, his round stomach lightly touching her. Then he pushed her. She fell back but stayed on her feet.

She looked fearful. The guy raised his thick arm to backhand her. Joyce looked at me. 'Uh, Ron. This is . . .'

'Ray,' I answered.

He glanced at me. 'Hi, Ray,' he said, not too unfriendly. He stared at Joyce coldly. 'We'll talk about this later.' He left, stomping on the carpet, and went into the other room.

Joyce and I were silent for a little while.

'What was that about?' I asked.

'Nevermind,' Joyce said, holding her arms.

She looked down at herself and shivered in the LA heat. I concentrated on breathing the smog-thick outside air.

From where we were on the porch I could see the Hollywood sign far off through the trees.

Fucking Hollywood.

Chapter Ten

THE PROUD AND THE SMUG

THE HOLLYWOOD HILLS looked over Los Angeles like kings to peasants. Hollywood could ruin people. Sherry went there guiltless and innocent and came out as Cherry Blossom, having forced sex with a frown. She had a sweet cheerleader face but she was fucking the quarterback for money. It really was too bad. Sickening. It broke my broken heart.

I needed a job. I needed it to keep my mind off people like Sherry and Helen, Joyce, Marta, Bill, and Don Gold and also to keep my mind off how little money I had.

That party ripped me up. Some fucking world we lived in. At this point, my life was going in one direction: job, depression, job, depression. The job fought off the depression with busywork but still a job was as slow and empty as free time.

I wasn't like other people. Other people could grin and bear it. They could applaud while watching some sex act, they could sweat and smile while lifting some warehouse box or unlocking some security door, or they could mingle their way through life like mad dogs. Their smiles came from cloud-high egos that they had for no reason at all. I would sit on a bus looking from passenger to passenger and they would all be self-absorbed, interested only in the space around them, their own view out the window, hoping no one sat next to them, annoyed that the guy behind them was breathing too heavy, or wondering if their hair was pressed right. People didn't look up. They wouldn't bother to look around to see that everyone on the bus was fat or ugly, or angry, and that nobody cared. I had a dream about a guy stabbing himself on the bus, screaming to death, shouting for help, and nobody was looking up, nobody helped him. He also happened to be walking a sheep wearing a party hat. Go figure. It was either a dream or a fantasy, just so I could prove my point, and finally know that I wasn't alone in my judgment.

Somehow people found it in themselves to grin and bear life. Jesus Christ, maybe everybody else was happy and content. As soon as I opened my mouth to smile I felt my mouth melting away.

And here I was, looking through the paper, looking for another job. Once upon a time I grew up in Silverlake, California in a small house with a half-dry lawn. I went to elementary school with all the other kids, played football on the cement playground and was pretty good, went on a camping trip where I snorkeled and saw yellow fish and somebody threw a dead skunk in the campfire. I went to high school among the dirty tan lockers that could be opened with a hard credit card, I went to math class where I stayed back in Algebra while most of the class went on to Geometry, I tried to drop out once, but then I stopped midway when I realized that there's really nowhere to go, I played football again, this time on a park lawn, but found I was too small and the kids were now playing tackle, I went back home and drank orange juice straight out of the refrigerator, made myself a sandwich of tomato, lettuce, and thinly sliced meat and ate it on the pepper-colored living room couch. I graduated in a blur, not really knowing anything, and in the end I put my gown back in a large cardboard box, and a girl named Samantha laughed at me because I was still wearing the hat. Then I got jobs, met women, fought with my parents who were getting divorced, got myself an apartment and for a moment I was almost proud, but that feeling lasted as long as a sitcom, and then I had some experiences, and I was living what they called life.

And once again I found myself looking through the classifieds like a No-man. I couldn't find anything with low experience so I went to check my mail as a distraction. I hadn't checked it in days.

There was only junk mail and a typed note from David, the writer who was also building manager, that said he would be moving out and so someone needed to fill the spot. As building manager you got your rent paid. This was very, very lucky. I even smiled.

I walked straight up the stairs to David's apartment and knocked twice. He opened the door shoeless with a wide, happy grin, holding a glass of white wine.

'Yes,' he said.

'I'm Ray, from downstairs.'

'Yes. I know.'

A pause. He stood there, smiling.

'I'm here about the building manager job.'

'Oh, right. Could you come back?' He looked behind him as if to find an excuse but there was nobody there. He looked back at me gravely. He didn't quite make my eye. 'I'll talk to you now,' he said.

I followed him into his apartment, which was twice the size of mine but cramped with moving boxes and furniture. Movie posters hung on the walls: *Manhattan*, *Raging Bull*, *Cabaret* and a movie called *Simon*. There was half a bottle of white wine sitting on a polished dining room table.

'There's nowhere for you to sit. Do you mind standing?'

'No.'

He sat in the only chair. He stared at me, slightly moving his eyes up and down over me.

'What do you need to know?' I asked.

'Have you ever managed an apartment?'

'No, but I've lived in them all my life.' I realized that was a dumb thing to say and forced a laugh like I meant it to be a joke. He just nodded. 'And I've lived in this building five years, longer than you even. And I know most everybody who lives here.'

'Why didn't you apply back when I was applying for the job?'

'I didn't know that it was available and I probably had a job back then.'

'You don't have a job?' he said with tired surprise, as if he didn't actually care that much.

'I have a few job offers that I'm deciding on right now.'

He looked at me, suddenly with hard skepticism.

'One is for a place that duplicates film. It's called Langford Films. Have you heard of it?'

'No.'

'I thought you would have, being that you're involved in film.'

I looked around at the posters on the walls and tilted my nose just high enough so it seemed like I knew more than him.

'No, I haven't heard of it,' he said with a certain amount of shame. He paused. 'Do you think you could handle the job of building manager?'

'Sure. But I mean, there can't be that much to do.'

'Well . . .'

'C'mon, there isn't *that* much.' I nudged him with my eyes.

He smiled. 'I'm sure you could handle it.'

He was a nice guy. I liked David.

'How many other applicants do you have?'

'A few,' he said, but I could tell he was lying. His eyes went to his wine glass. 'Leave me your number and I'll get back to you.'

We stood silently for a moment, two men in a standoff.

'Anything else?' I said.

'No.'

'Why are you leaving anyway?'

'I . . . uh . . . got a job.'

'What kind of job?'

'I sold a screenplay,' he said. Partly with pride, partly with defeat because he knew that wasn't exactly like getting a job. And maybe the guy who lifted boxes or unlocked doors for a living might resent him for it.

'Oh yeah?' I said.

'Yeah.'

'They're going to make it?'

'Yes.'

'Congratulations.'

'Thank you,' he said. He tried holding back a proud smile. But his upper lip twitched away from his bottom lip and the smile came.

'If you don't mind me asking, how much do you make on something like that?'

His face lit up a question mark.

'Paying you,' I said.

'A lot.'

'A lot. Like a hundred thousand dollars?'

He got up and began walking me towards the door.

'More than that,' he said.

'More? Really? Like how much?'

His lips came away from his teeth to show an even larger smile. I could tell he didn't care that much about salary etiquette, he liked giving out this figure: 'One million dollars.'

'One mil—'

'I'll call you about the job,' he said.

He was grinning full now, the pride and the smug coming back to him.

He shut the door and I was left in the hallway. I stood looking straight at the door, speechless. I had misjudged David. I didn't think he was the kind of guy who would so quickly eat up a million dollars with a proud Hollywood smile. But he had fallen into the walk-of-fame abyss. He was tainted like so many others.

Here I was groveling for a job that paid my rent, and David, a million dollars in his pocket, was questioning me about the apartment manager's job like I was the criminal. There wasn't anything wrong with me. I had some morals. He was the one who was making too much money for too little work, while the warehouse slobs were busy getting dirty and angry, then shelling out eight dollars for a couple hours of nothing much, feeding David's proud wallet. I wasn't the criminal. He was. Goddamnit, *he* was.

The depression was getting thicker. I got a job in a restaurant parking lot, taking money and finding keys. I won't even talk about it that much because it's embarrassing. The way I was now, the job was about all I could handle.

I even tried writing Helen again but I was too paralyzed and nothing came. I had seen too much gone wrong. Coming from her, Sherry, David. I wrote:

Dear Helen,
I love you.

But then I stopped because I didn't love her. I didn't love anything. I was afraid that maybe I was incapable of love. In the middle of that thought, for the briefest of seconds, I considered that I should find religion. Put my faith in something other than people. It helped criminals and the poor, maybe it could help me. But that didn't last long. Then I thought that I should go up to Helen, confess to the letter writing. Maybe she'd be sympathetic. The whole ordeal might bring us closer together. I lied a picture to myself of the two of us holding hands. None of this seemed like an option.

I came home from the parking lot, tired from all the slowness. The phone was ringing. I picked up.

'Ray,' said Marta's voice.

I felt something for her right away.

'Hi, Marta.'

'How have you been?' she asked.

'I've been OK.'

'Yeah? That's good,' she said cheerily. Man, I just couldn't shed how much I liked her voice. I still wanted her, her warm safety and calming smile.

'How's Bill?' I asked.

'Why do you have to bring him up every time we talk?'

'I don't know. Instinct.'

'He's fine, if you knew him,' she said bitterly.

'Fine.'

'Anyway, that's partially why I'm calling.'

I felt a twinge of hope. Maybe Bill was dead.

No. 'Bill's throwing me a party for my birthday,' she said.

'It's your birthday?'

'You know when my birthday is, don't you?' she asked, maybe a little sad longing in her voice.

'Yeah. It's in a couple of weeks. Little soon for a party, isn't it?'

'Well, Bill's going out of town for a few weeks so he wanted to throw it before he left.'

She said that last sentence all full of new friendship pride.

'Do I have to bring a gift?'

'If you want to,' she said, wink-wink.

'I'll try and make it.'

'Please do. You remember we're still friends, right?'

'Yeah, I remember.' Her gruff Marta sweetness made me sad.

I remembered last year's birthday. Marta and I went to a bar deep in Hollywood, right next to the studios, filled with old Hollywood veterans. The place was half empty, full of blue neon, and had naked paintings of bunny-like women on the walls. Marta and I laughed and smiled as we got drunk watching the sad patrons telling stories to anybody who would listen. 'I knew Marilyn Monroe when she was Norma Jean. A friend of mine did one of her first screen tests.' That kind of thing. We drank until shutdown and then walked as far as we could towards the beach before we passed out on a bus-stop bench until sunrise.

The birthday before that we spent on the beach and watched two pale bums fucking in the tunnel under the Pacific Coast Highway until the cops came and took them away because there were kids on the beach watching too. That year I bought her salt and pepper shakers, real ones, the kind you found in a diner, because she said as a kid there never were any in her house and she didn't know why. She liked that gift.

The year before that we spent apart and the years before that I can't quite remember because my memory doesn't go back far enough. She was probably with those old boyfriends who beat her and locked her indoors.

'It's on Saturday, around nine o'clock. Bring somebody . . . if you like. Dress any way you want.'

'Yeah, OK.'

That was two days away.

'Do you think you can make it?' she said.

'I'm not sure.'

'I hope you can.'

'Hey, Marta,' I asked, 'when's the last time anyone ever threw you a party?'

'I can't remember. I don't think anybody ever has.'

'Don't forget that,' I said.

'OK, Ray, I won't.'

Chapter Eleven

CARL'S JR STAR

AS MUCH AS I didn't want to see Joyce again, I didn't want to go to Marta's party alone. Joyce was pretty enough to make Marta jealous. When I called her up, she asked if it was OK if Sherry came along. I wanted to say no but I also had a strange desire to see Sherry again. I'd never seen someone so beautiful and so destroyed. Someone without a scratch or a blemish, but then again marked beyond repair. I needed to see if she really was an angel who had fallen down to hell. And I thought if I brought Joyce and Sherry together, Marta might see the light about me.

I wore my best clothes. I put on my blue pants which looked almost like slacks and an off-white button-down shirt with a pattern of tiny orange and red checkers. I almost looked decent. I wanted to make an impression on Marta. I wasn't a loser who quit or got fired from jobs, a man who just took keys for a living. I was good, the kind of person who did the firing.

Joyce insisted on driving. I tried to change her mind but she said she had to drive. She explained. 'I can't be a passenger. I just can't.' She wouldn't say why. I gave in to her slight look of terror. But this way I couldn't escape the party by the wheel of my own car.

I knew everything wasn't going to go well when Joyce picked me up in her car and Sherry was sitting in the back seat with Don Gold. He shook my hand through the space between the front seats and said, 'Hello' with a dead expression. 'Roy, is it?'

'Ray.'

'Sorry. Ray.'

Sherry was tucked in the back seat, her leg pressed against his. She was wearing small, slender black jeans and a soft blue sweater. Don was dressed for a coke binge night on the town. He wore a V-neck T-shirt that showed off some slight chest hairs poking through and a black vinyl jacket.

'I didn't think you'd ever call me again,' Joyce said. 'You seemed so mad after the last party.'

'I'm not used to parties.'

'I see.'

'This is more parties in a row than I've been to in all my life,' I said. 'Marta's my friend so I had to go.'

Joyce smiled and clutched the steering wheel.

'This is a birthday party, right?' she asked.

'Yeah.'

'Did you get her anything?'

'No.'

'Why not?'

'She's got enough already,' I said.

'Oh, I feel bad. We should get her something.'

'She gets enough from her boyfriend.'

'Who's her boyfriend?' asked Sherry.

'Some guy in the music industry,' I said without looking back at her.

'He must be rich if he lives where I think he lives,' she said.

The party was being held at Bill's house high in the Pacific Palisades hills. We were ascending the winding curves of Sunset Boulevard. Joyce's driving was worrying me. She stared at the road like she was studying it. That is, like she didn't quite know what was in front of her.

'We should stop off and get her something,' Joyce said.

'Well, here's a liquor store. Let's stop and get her some beer.'

Joyce gave me a defeated look.

'We're almost there,' I said. 'She'll be fine without a gift.'

Joyce gave up and started smiling again.

Joyce turned off Sunset. We were ten numbers away. The houses were getting larger and more protected by trees the further we went up the hill. I could see the ocean behind us. The tall, two- and three-story houses looked down at our car like angry Wall Street buildings. We pulled in front of Bill's house. We must have been early. There were only four cars parked in front of the house.

Bill's house was part cheap stucco and part stone, the equivalent of the gold chain he hung around his hairy, brown neck – part wealth, part bad taste. At first I was angry as we walked through the front door which had a knocker of a dragon. Sherry and Joyce were locked arm in arm, looking up and around. Then, I had to admit, I was a little jealous when I saw that the back of his house was a solid wall of glass looking out on the LA city lights. Marta's made it, I thought. But then I saw Bill. He was holding a drink in a thick glass and talking to someone who looked much like him, tailored and clean, but dirty like grit under white fingernails.

Bill was a high-class criminal. There were posters on the walls for singing groups that I didn't listen to because they were all so bad. Teenage boy groups, black or white, shiny and cute, which made easy millions. Almost like a crooked get-rich-quick scheme. There were a few gold and platinum records by the front doorway. They were the first thing a person saw when they entered the house.

Bill was laughing now. He needed some kind of ill-treatment. He was false and unnatural, gleaming teeth and tanning-salon skin. And the gold chain. He was attractive only because he had money. The hair was so thick on his dark hands it needed combing. Only people like me knew the truth, the people of the real world, the people without a glass balcony that they thought gave them vision. The vision was mine.

Marta came up to me smiling, looking real good, hooped earrings and a black dress that came down in a triangle between her breasts, fancier than I'd ever seen her.

I was prepared for this moment. Both of my feet were planted firm on the ground.

'Marta, this is Joyce and Sherry and Don,' I said, equal parts proud and cold.

Everybody said their hellos. 'Happy Birthday's went around. Marta didn't look jealous or stricken. All she looked was happy. She was pure, drugless happy.

Instantly, I didn't want to be there. I went into the living room and sat by myself on one of the black leather couches which surrounded a glass table. From where I was sitting I could see the front door, the kitchen, the dining room and all the people I brought with me starting to laugh and mingle.

Sherry was looking exceptionally bright. She started talking to the man who looked like Bill and she looked up at him like daughter to father. She was full of bright admiration. The guy was happy too, proud to be talking to such a perfect, young thing. The pride was all tucked into the sides of his smile.

More people steadily came in the front door. I didn't know any of them and I was sure Marta didn't either. She shook all their hands and smiled brightly. I watched her walk around like she was looking for something and then spot me on the couch. She raised her head like she had found it when she found me and came over.

'I was looking for you,' she said.

'You were?' I said without enthusiasm.

'I wanted to see you.'

'Why?'

'I haven't seen you for a long time,' she said, like it was obvious.

'That was your choice, not mine.'

'Ray, you know that's not true.'

'We've both got our own things going, I guess.'

'It's great to see you with somebody. She seems nice. And that other girl is beautiful. Bill's friend Dennis recognized her from one of her movies. Do you know anything about that?'

'About what?'

'Her movies?'

'No.'

'Neither do I.'

I was glad she didn't.

She looked up to nowhere, chewing her lip like she did. We sat in silence for a few minutes while she looked around at her party and I looked at her, trying not to feel attracted to her. Then she said excitedly, 'Do you know who's going to be here?'

'No.'

'John McTiernan.'

'Who's that?'

'He's the one who directed those *Die Hard* movies I think.'

'Why?'

'I don't know. Bill knows him from somewhere.'

What I meant was, why did he direct those *Die Hard* movies?

'How are you doing?' she asked, plastic-cheery.

'I'm fine.'

'You have fun tonight, Ray,' she ordered.

'All right.'

Her eyes were suddenly bright. 'Did you bring me a gift?' She said.

'Yeah,' I lied. 'I put it on the table with the others.'

There was a table right by the front door covered with wrapped boxes small and large. There was an extra-large box sitting on the floor next to the table about the size of a large-screen TV. If it was a large-screen TV there was no way she could fit it into her small house. Unless Bill was buying her a new house too.

'I can't wait to see what you got me,' she said. 'I have to go, though. I have *so* many people to talk to. There are so many *interesting* people here.' The old Marta I knew would have hated the way she was talking. 'You have fun, all right?'

'Right.'

Marta went away and I was left on the couch for the rest of

the night. I didn't feel like going anywhere. There was no one *interesting* here. I sat on the black couch the whole party.

About two hours in, a couple came up to me and asked if I read fortunes. The woman, thin and pretty, said, 'You look so peaceful sitting there. I thought you were a fortune teller.'

'You got any tarot cards,' said her uglier boyfriend.

She said, 'You look wise in an angry, fucked-up sort of way.'

I stared at her.

'Oops,' she giggled. 'But you really should smile more.'

They laughed, locked arms and walked away. I tried wincing a smile. I kept it ten minutes until my cheekbones ached. Look, I'm enjoying myself, I thought.

I got up once to go to the bathroom. I asked Bill where it was. He didn't even look at me when he told me. He pointed, 'Over there, to the left,' and went on talking to a girl who Joyce had told me was a famous singer when we first got to the party. I didn't recognize her. Supposedly there were a lot of famous people here.

There was a line waiting outside the bathroom door. Three people, two women and one guy stood outside. The women were short, blond, with blue star-struck eyes. The guy had thin lips and a sharp nose. They were all darker than dirt.

'You don't have to cut it with a razor blade,' he was saying. 'It's not like cocaine.'

'I know someone who ate a poppy plant and got just as high,' said the taller girl. You couldn't tell the women apart except by height. 'You just eat out the inside.'

'That's a pure opium high.'

'You can do that?' said the shorter girl.

'Sure you can,' he said. 'You know, it's the California flower.'

They all looked heavy serious.

I wished these people would shut up. I had to go to the bathroom.

Joyce walked out of the bathroom but didn't see me standing there. She walked past me. The three people walked in. Five minutes later they came out. They were rubbing their noses, eyes glazed, smiling slyly. I walked inside. There was a thin film of dust of heroin by the sink and a rolled up dollar bill which they'd left. The bathroom was made of black tile. The sink was marble. I'd never seen this before but there was a black toilet. For some reason that impressed me more than anything. And I wasn't in the mood to be impressed. I pissed, flushed and the toilet filled up blue. When I walked out, the couple who had asked me if I was a fortune teller were waiting. They didn't recognize me. I went back to the couch.

Marta was opening the presents. She opened the big box first because she *just* couldn't wait. It was a large-screen TV. 'Oh my,' she screamed in a little girl way. The rest of the gifts were perfumes, soaps, and books of the usual sort. She didn't seem to notice that I didn't leave her a gift.

Sherry ended up going home with Bill's friend Dennis. He was from Hollywood and she was a young starlet. No matter how much she said she had contempt for Hollywood, he could get her places. She was a piece of meat like the Carl's Jr star. Six million sold. The quest for fame and money seemed like it could kill people. It had sure gotten to Sherry. It had gotten to everybody here, so proud to be at this celebrity party. Sherry and Bill's friend flirted throughout the night. I watched them from the couch clutching and kissing. She locked her arm in his, eyeing his gold watch, his version of Bill's gold chain. Slimy as ice.

Joyce pleaded with me throughout the night to get off the couch and join her. She spent most of her time with Don Gold. He didn't seem to mind that Sherry had gone off with someone else. They tried talking to other people at the party but then, Joyce flustered, they ended up talking to each other.

Joyce finally did end up meeting another guy, a short, small-eyed man in his forties with whom she had a good time, forcing laughter. He was ugly but wore a sharp, checkered suit.

I sat on the couch, cold, dark and lifeless, waiting for my ride to take me home.

When that time came, Joyce looked down at me like I had ruined her night.

'Do you need a ride?' she said bitterly.

'Yes.'

'Well, I'm going with Jeffrey. You can sit in the back if you want.'

Jeffrey stood next to Joyce. He was about six inches shorter than her, balding heavily, and he stared at me with eager, drug-smiling eyes.

'Yeah, I'll do that,' I said.

Joyce wasn't expecting I'd say that. She gave me a cold but confused stare.

I guessed Joyce was drunk enough to not mind if somebody else did the driving. I felt a little better on the ride home. The wind blew hard in my face. Jeffrey asked me if it was all right if the window was open but I didn't answer. I sat in the cramped back seat smelling the old car smell and concentrating on the air blowing in my face until my eyes teared and my hair looked like Beethoven's. Jeffrey had his hand on Joyce's thigh. He said, 'You're very beautiful.' He couldn't wait to get her home.

Joyce replied, 'Thank you,' in a disinterested way.

'I swear I've seen you somewhere before,' he said more than once as we made our way down Sunset. I knew exactly where he'd seen her. He would be in for a shock.

They dropped me off and I left them with quiet goodbyes.

Chapter Twelve

GOD DOESN'T DRIVE IN A LIMOUSINE

WHEN I GOT back to the apartment, late, around 4 a.m., I had an urge to write Helen another letter.

I felt a sudden longing now, even stronger than when I was at the college. I could just picture her opening the letter the way she had that day when I watched her. I could see the impact it would have on her and the people around her. Her feelings would be strong – fear, maybe, or guilt – and those feelings would be because of me.

I wrote the letter in the faint light of one desk lamp.

It's me again. Thought you'd lost me? Impossible. I'm here for the long haul. And you're trapped here with me like a prison visitor.

I was in your room. Or do you know that? I tried not to leave a trace. I saw those stained sheets on your bed. Why doesn't it sicken you when you moan like that, your ass to the air? It sickens me. There's something very wrong with the way people act. I'm the only one with any sense because I get angry. Can you understand that? I bet you can't.

Anyway, I still watch you around campus. But I've given up on you a little bit. I heard you told security about me. You shouldn't have done that. It just makes me work harder not to get caught and so they'll never find me.

I hope someday we can be together. When that day comes we can stain your sheets like those I saw in your room. I know

you'll come around. I'm certain of it. One day we will finally
be together and we'll ride off into the fucking sunset.

I wrote and wrote late that night and wound up falling asleep on
the desk as the sun was coming up. Tomorrow I would drop the
letter in the mailbox far away from Venice, at a different postmark.
I'd probably go to Hollywood and drop it in a mailbox close to
where I knew another security guard lived.

When I woke up the next day, the light on the desk had faded
out completely.

The first thing I did was reread the letter to Helen that lay
under me on the desk. There was something very wrong with
it. It said all the things I wanted to say but it was aimless, it
would get me nowhere. I knew I would never truly have Helen.
That confused me. There had to be something else I could do.
Not only about getting Helen, but something to show people –
everybody – right and wrong. To show people how life should be
lived. I could write Helen all I wanted but that was only between
me and her. There was so much damage in the world and all
of it needed to be fixed. The Martas, the Sherrys, the Davids,
the Helens. And those were only the people I'd met. The whole
world was collapsing with misplaced devotion. Thinking about
that point, even my pen was at a loss for words. One could call
it writer's block.

I checked the clock. The bright clock radio gleamed twelve
noon. I was four hours late for work. I called in sick.

I was back to daytime TV.

I watched a talk show about celebrity marriages. Now, there were
some people who had no hold on reality. At least if one of them
was married to a mortal, they'd know what it was like to look at
a normal face everyday, not one always caked over with glitter
and sheen. Celebrities who were married to each other were on
another world as far as I was concerned, so far removed from
life you could say they had touched a little piece of God. So

much security and respect they didn't even know what to do with it. Sure they might have had problems, but people knew who they were.

And here I was sitting in my trailer-park apartment, home, lying sick from a parking lot job, rejected by women, and someone on TV, a close friend of a star, was saying, 'They just got back from a relaxing vacation in the Caribbean. You know, they have so many pressures, sometimes they just have to unwind.'

'I can imagine. I can imagine,' said the host. 'The pressures of stardom must get to them.'

'He's taking a break just before he starts work on a new movie with producer Joseph Silverman. It's going to be a great detective film in the forties' tradition.'

They were talking about Tim Griffith and his wife Robin Culver. America's most adored couple.

'The big news is that on the vacation they conceived a child.'

Everyone in the audience applauded.

'They got a dog just to test themselves out.'

The audience laughed.

Damn, if only. If only when I bought a dog people would care enough to laugh. If only people gave a shit about anything I ever did. Just then, Tim Griffith and his wife came out and the audience exploded. Tim Griffith stood in front of the audience and they cheered and shrieked for him like he was money they were about to receive.

'How are you?' asked the host with an almost sexy smile.

'I'm fine,' he smiled back.

'So, what—' she stopped and took a breath. 'I'm tongue-tied,' she said. The audience laughed and applauded again. 'So, tell me about your vacation.'

'It was beautiful. We stayed in a cabana for fourteen days. I learned to scuba dive.'

'What, wasn't Bel-Air nice enough for you?' More laughter. More smiles.

Damn it. Either that kind of life was meant for me more than I could imagine, or I was stuck in this basement for the rest of my life. What was life if you were nothing? If no one knew who you were, and even if they did know you, they'd sleep with a guy like Bill and feel nothing.

A person needed respect. Celebrities, as fake and tainted as they were, they had respect. Most people didn't have respect. I didn't have respect. Marta didn't have any respect for herself or from anybody. Sherry had the wrong kind of respect. She got respect for fucking. None of the people I ever worked with had respect. And those people who nobody cared about but their aging mother were giving me the assuming looks. 'Are you a fortune teller?' Laugh. They'd give me respect. Soon, their respect would turn to awe. Everybody, including Marta, would know that I was a man of pride and worth.

That's when I knew exactly what I needed. I needed fame of my own. I couldn't be nobody forever. It was killing me. To be unknown was to not exist, and that was the same as death. The best way to get fame was to touch fame, get close to it, show it what mattered and what didn't, make it realize the things it didn't know. After that, I'd be rolling in more respect than celebrities had money.

And in the process I could show everybody what was right and good. Show them that all their blind pornography and gold-chain devotion was wrong.

Tim Griffith was a good target. He was greedy for Hollywood like David upstairs and on that talk show he answered questions with a sly, slimy smile like Bill. He was everything wrong with this cold entertainment world. Everyone was concentrating on show-ing themselves off. Griffith was king of that kind of people.

Griffith was the world's most beloved star. That meant he was the world's most out-of-touch. The more famous he got, the less he deserved it. When there was so much suffering going on, it seemed the more Griffith got wealthy and well-liked, the less it made any sense. I could find him and show him the right way of the world.

Because Griffith was so famous, he was an important figure. If I could change him, people would follow. The celebrity cult. It was wrong but that's how people acted. Who knows, maybe I could change everybody, from the top to the bottom. Maybe I could change the world.

I didn't know much about Tim Griffith. I'd seen a couple of his films. Big, fake, happy-ending movies. Griffith had no idea how much he caused the things I despised. Hollywood was all surface and misplaced devotion, everything that had made Marta and Sherry and Helen go wrong. Helen and Marta chose their high-class friends. Sherry was destroyed by Hollywood. She came there as an innocent, only to fuck people at parties so she could get ahead in her starlet world. And the Hollywood world fucked me in its own way. While I was busy taking keys and lifting boxes, Hollywood ran its business with gleamy pride. They were telling the world everything was all right while the business of suffering and the business of bad feeling ran through everything.

And what did Tim Griffith know about any of this? He could cough and the audience would applaud. What did he know about lifting boxes or turning keys for a living, or about seeing innocence destroyed?

Maybe if he'd married a civilian he would seem more human. But he didn't. His wife, Robin, was just as glossy and perfect. She didn't seem to have the least bit of distaste for what they were doing up on stage, smiling and accepting the audiences' worship.

Well, worship this, Mr Griffith. I am the man who will show you the way. I am your connection to the real world. Like a priest who can relay the peasant's message to and from God. But I will show you that you are not God. God wouldn't ignore what is right in life. God wouldn't forget that people die on the streets. God would not let people fuck for money. God would not have so much while other people have so little. God would not smile out of his twinkling eyes for profit. God's every blink would not be worth a thousand dollars. And God would not drive in a limousine.

It was easy for me to get close to the movies. Hell, I lived in LA, I might as well have used it.

When I wrote the first letter, I sat at my desk in the living room with the sound of *Entertainment Tonight* high-volume in the background. Like Helen's letters, I wrote it on my lime-green portable typewriter. First I'd write them by hand and then I'd type them up so there wouldn't be any mistakes. I started the letter: 'Dear student.'

You don't know me yet, but you will soon know me well, if not by name. Perhaps we could become friends. I have something to offer you, something I think you need to know. You better take notice of me because I am going to be with you for a long time.

I wouldn't exactly call myself a fan. But if being a fan means applauding shallowness, being out of touch with the real world, looking pretty for money, being unaware of the hearts that are broken across the globe, well then, sir, I am your number one fan.

We can have ourselves a healthy relationship. God knows I haven't seen many healthy relationships but I think we can be good for each other. You can offer me change and maybe some hope that the world isn't doomed and drowning. I can show you good ways. If you change I'll know people can be saved. If you don't, I can't say what's going to happen.

I know your kind well. I know your habits. I've seen many people like you, so many that it seems like the world is being overrun by the superficial and the thoughtless, your children. I know all about what controls you and who you control. People would die for you, I know that. In some ways you have more control than the President. We both know that you are more famous than God. That's why, and I think you'll agree, you have to be stopped.

I watched a talk show you were on with your wife. Why doesn't it sicken you to smile in front of all those people? They suck your cock with their clapping hands. I know you looked out at those fat housewives with disgust. You thought they were beneath you. They are slow, fat, and stupid, while your white teeth gleam, your blue eyes shine, and you work hard for your million dollars. What you don't know is that those women get beaten by their husbands who come home from shoveling shit for a day. I see you with all your pretty smiles and become boiling with rage. What else can I do?

Maybe those housewives' daughters go out to Hollywood and sell their pussies. I don't like these people either. That's something we can agree on. That's where we are probably alike. What you don't understand is that you are nothing more than them. In fact, you are the cause of their kind. Those daughters wouldn't be fucking up a storm if they didn't see you making an easy million dollars with a pretty face. Those housewives wouldn't be so fat and stupid if they weren't so busy worshipping false idols. You, my friend, are the Golden Calf. Decadence and shallowness, threatening and ruining the people.

Now, I bet you didn't know that people struggle through life while you film movies, or spend weekends in the Caribbean, or whatever the fuck you do. But people live miserable lives. People get fucked over by people they love, or get fucked up the ass by people they don't, or work in a warehouse with morons. But you don't have any idea about any of that. Let's just call you Mr Out-of-touch. And if you haven't guessed it yet, I am here to teach you. Believe me, in the end we'll both be better off. People will know who I am and people will understand what you're not.

Sincerely,
Someone who knows

I had another paragraph where I threatened him a lot, but I wanted to be taken seriously first, not just someone who threw out a threat, but someone who had stuff on his mind.

I folded the letter in a plain, white envelope, like Helen's letters, and sealed it.

I remembered from the talk show that Griffith's new movie was being produced by Joseph Silverman, the guy who did all the action movies. I called information and asked for Joseph Silverman. Easy, they gave me the number. I went to the pay phone right outside my door and dialed the number. A girl answered, 'Joseph Silverman's office.' Her voice was young and sweet. I imagined red fingernails.

'Hello?' she said after I didn't say anything. I was surprised I'd reached the office.

'Hi, I'm in Bel-Air trying to deliver a package to Tim Griffith but I'm lost.'

'Who is this?'

'This is Jerry. I'm a messenger.' I used my father's name.

'Hold on,' she said and then called to someone else, 'Isn't Tim Griffith staying at his home in Malibu during filming?' There was some talking that I couldn't hear and then she said, 'He's not in Bel-Air. He's at his beach house.'

'Are you sure? I was told to come here.'

'I don't know why. He's not there.'

'1700 Watercress, right?'

She ruffled some pages. 'No, that's 610 Donaldson Road.'

'Huh. No wonder I'm lost.' I laughed.

'Someone gave you the wrong directions.'

'You might as well give me the address to his beach house in case he's not in Bel-Air.'

'OK. That's 1520 Mountainview Terrace.'

'1520 Mountainview?'

'Yes. Terrace.'

'Well, thanks a lot. Hope I didn't inconvenience you.'

'Fine. Hope you make it,' she said a little bitterly. 'B-bye.'

I hung up and walked back into my apartment. I had called for one address and came out with two.

Chapter Thirteen

MR OUT-OF-TOUCH

I PUT ON blue work pants and a light-blue button-down shirt and headed for 1520 Mountainview Terrace. I didn't just want to send the letter through the mail, I wanted to see where I was sending it.

I drove on PCH towards his Malibu home, past sliding mountains and tall houses along the beach. Mountainview Terrace was more secluded than most of the beach-house streets. I checked the Thomas Brothers Map and Mountainview was only four houses long.

There was an open gate which guarded the small beach-house town. The gate was probably closed at night. There wasn't a guard. I parked my car near the gate and walked along the houses. Dressed as neat as I was, I looked less like a stranger than if I showed up on his doorstep in my old, beat-up car.

I couldn't see very much of the houses from the street. They were all hidden behind thick white walls and trees. I could only see the roof and a few windows. I tried looking in the windows but I was too far away. I could only see the reflection of the trees.

When I got to Griffith's house, I saw that his was the nicest of the row. It was surrounded by chin-high adobe walls. Through the trees – orange, apple and avocado – I could see a piece of the Spanish tile roof, smooth and new, stained a little by the overhanging trees. The house was more of an estate than a simple beach home. There were three separate buildings that I could make out. There was the main building, which was already bigger than the other beach houses, a second building which was small but two stories, a guest house I imagined, and then a third one, very small, but I couldn't imagine what it was.

There was a black BMW, four doors, parked in the driveway, close to the street. They were probably home so I didn't want it to seem like I was checking them out. Finding the mailbox was easy. It was attached to the garage, next to the black, dead-bolted front gate. Through the gate I could see a red tiled path which led to the front door, obscured by flowers and trees.

I dropped the letter into the mailbox, walked away briskly and thought, 'This is wealth.' Worse than Marta's Bill. Pure decadence.

Writing Griffith wasn't like writing Helen. I wanted to meet Helen but she turned on me. Griffith was never any good. He wouldn't ever be able to live in a house like that in good conscience if he was any good. I wanted to show him how real people lived, in basement apartments and unloved, the widespread unhappiness of the world. His beach-house wealth would mean nothing if he had real-world guilt hanging over him. He didn't deserve to be living there, sitting pretty, high above strife. No one deserved to live that well.

It was the rich people who didn't know anything about the world, and it was the celebrities who were adored only for being pretty. Celebrities were criminal on two counts. People like Sherry, Marta and I got caught in their wake.

For one second I thought, 'Christ, I shouldn't be doing this.' I took one step toward the mailbox to retrieve the letter. But then I thought, 'No, he deserves it.' If he wasn't going to share the wealth, at least I could share the grief.

I drove away from Griffith's beach house full of thought. Griffith was going to be a hard man to change because his corruption was so far along. I wanted him to change, just like I wanted everyone to change, but I knew it was going to be difficult and bitter work. I still sheltered some optimism. The world wasn't collapsing. Love still existed. People could change. But seeing Griffith's Malibu home made me wonder if bad minds and bad motives were already too firmly rooted in the ground, like a tree in cement.

I drove on PCH as quick as I could through the traffic. Next I wanted to see his Bel-Air home. Maybe I'd sneak a peek inside. He wasn't supposed to be there.

When I got to the Bel-Air home I saw that I wasn't the only one looking. A pair of out-of-towners, husband and wife, were staring at 610 Donaldson Road, pointing and taking pictures. They were both wearing white shorts. He was wearing a light-blue tennis shirt and hers was pink. I walked up to the front gate, solid and black, and rang the doorbell. The couple watched me like I was a king. I rang the bell again but there was no answer. 'Guess he's not home,' I said to the house. The house was old and brick, painted white. The dusty red of the bricks seeped through the white paint. The house made me angrier than the summer home because it wasn't concealed, I could see everything. It was enormous, like a castle. There had to be forty bedrooms. It was surrounded by a well-groomed, avocado-green lawn. There was an archway next to a side entrance wide enough for three limousines. The house loomed over the street saying, 'Money brought me happiness.' Every house on the street was enormous but again, like the beach house, none were so nice as Griffith's. The others looked like big versions of small houses. But Griffith's looked like a mansion and a mansion alone.

I took a step away from the house. The couple were staring at me.

'Do you know him?' the husband asked.

I heard him clearly but I said, 'Excuse me?'

'Do you know Tim Griffith?'

'I was supposed to pick up a package but it doesn't look like he's home. Maybe they're at the beach house.'

'He has a beach house?' said the wife with deep-stricken awe.

Then it occurred to me. 'How did you get this address?'

'I have a cousin who works in the movies,' the husband said proudly. 'He said he would give me the address if all I did was look. He didn't want me pestering Mr Griffith. We're visiting from out of town.'

'Oh really? Where you from?'

'Utah.'

'You Mormons?'

'Yes,' they both said at the same time.

'Aren't Mormons not supposed to watch movies?'

'Oh, not us,' said the wife. 'We're not like that.'

'I don't know what I would do without movies,' said her husband.

'Oh yeah?'

'Tim Griffith movies especially,' he said. 'I love the one about the cross-country car race, *Highway Fire*. I've always had fantasies about being a race car driver. You know, on the drive over I pushed our little car here up to ninety-five on the open road.' He chuckled.

The little wife smiled. 'Oh, honey, don't brag.'

'You're pathetic,' I thought.

'I didn't think the car could do it.' He paused. 'I must have seen *Highway Fire* four or five times.'

They continued staring at the house.

'What do you do for a living?' I asked.

'Me? I'm a welder.'

'You weld things? What kind of things do you weld?'

'Well, all kinds of things. Mainly I weld pipes for plumbing or steel rods for buildings. Basically.'

'So that job must get pretty hot.'

'Hot?'

'After a day's work you must be sweaty and achy.'

'Sure. That's part of the job.'

'Now,' I said, finger in the air, 'do you think Tim Griffith knows anything about hard labor? He might play a guy who works hard or goes to war or something, but what do you think he knows about suffering?'

'I . . . I don't know. I just like his movies.'

'You like his movies.'

'I don't know anything about what you're saying.'

He looked forlorn, shuffling his feet like a child lost, as if he didn't know what to believe.

'Tim Griffith doesn't know about suffering. The kind of hell-suffering you and I go through every day.'

My hands were in my pockets, feet planted firm.

'I think Tim Griffith is a fine actor,' he stated. 'He does a service to the community.'

'The community? Whose community?'

'Yours and mine.'

'You mean the community that slaves day to day in grease so that on the weekend they can spend more on a movie than they would for a meal, to finance his home.' I pointed at the home like a prosecutor points at the defendant.

The husband and his wife were cowering back a little. But I could see I got them with that last statement. I could change people.

'Don't you just maybe think there's something wrong with this Tim Griffith. I mean, he's getting paid millions to race around in cars and live in that house and have his happy life. And all the while you try and drive fast in your little, what's that, an Escort?'

'Yes.'

'While you're off fantasizing, Tim Griffith is off making movies for more money than you'll ever see. He doesn't give a shit about you.'

'I really don't know, sir. I just like his movies. I—'

'All the while the world is going to hell.'

'Mister, I—' he looked towards the house as if it would give him some moral support. 'I think Tim Griffith is a fine man,' he said sadly.

'You don't know now, but you'll see.'

I looked over at the house. It looked more sickly and daunting than ever. The red of the bricks seemed to be seeping through the white paint like blood.

The couple stared at me fearfully as I left. I told them I had a screenplay to deliver to Clint Eastwood. They didn't know how to take that. Four blocks away from the house, I saw in my rear-view mirror that they were back to staring at the house and pointing. It might take time, but they'd learn. I was like a professor. I'd give them the greatest lesson in ethics that the ethicless city of Los Angeles had ever seen.

Chapter Fourteen

CANON FODDER

I WANTED TO know as much as I could about Tim Griffith. I wanted to know who I was going to control, who I was going to instruct. If I was going to be a teacher, I needed to educate myself. I rented the four movies of his that I knew about. I asked the high school girl at the video store about Tim Griffith movies and she found me a couple I hadn't heard of. 'Are you having a festival?' she asked.

'You could call it that,' I said.

I rented a second VCR so I could make copies of the movies for myself.

The first movie I watched was the movie that got him started and made him a star, *Trying Times*. I figured I'd watch them in the order they were released so I could see the influence he was slowly having on people. *Trying Times* was all about a kid in high school who can't get anywhere with girls. At first he's a loner, but in the end all of the girls love him. This movie might sound like a perfect example of how corrupt Griffith was, showing a false fantasy world, but I actually liked the movie. He was young when he made the movie so I couldn't fault him too much. At that point he was a pawn in somebody else's game. Maybe a producer or a director. I liked it all except for the scene which made him famous. Most everybody has watched the scene. In the cafeteria he starts singing to a certain girl. Everyone in the cafeteria stops to watch him. What was so special about the scene was that he actually sang the song right there. Usually they piped in somebody else's voice because most actors can't sing. But in the cafeteria scene, Griffith sang it himself. The audience thought the scene was so genuine that they loved him for it. He was an overnight success. His pictures were plastered everywhere. I remembered when the craze hit. You couldn't take a step without seeing his clean, smiling face. At the end of the song, Griffith gets up on the table and takes off his shirt and all the girls scream. He picks up a sugar dispenser and begins stroking it and shoving it between his legs like it's a penis. Griffith's career started with sex. As debasing as Marta in bed with Bill, Sherry in bed in front of a crowd. In fact, that teenage movie which everyone thought was so cute and harmless was responsible for Sherry lying on that bed. People couldn't do anything but fuck because all they had on their minds was sex. It all started with Griffith because he was in the mainstream, some sick sex-god hero. Once something was in the mainstream it's influence trickled lower and lower until it hit the bottom. Griffith's career was made by sex. I watched that scene five times in a row. I studied every move. I imagined little girls screaming in the movie theater at his cute teenage body. Those girls were soon to be corrupted as well, giggling and screaming in bed like they did for Griffith on screen. That scene all about sex laid the foundation for a future of power and undeserved riches.

The second movie I watched was called *A Kingdom of Trenches*. I'd seen this movie before but never had it meant so much as it did this time. The movie was all about preaching war and more dumb sex. It followed a platoon in World War I who were all quietly in love with each other, bonding like hell, and taking their shirts off every chance they got. They all had the same haircut and the same bright smile. They fought and they drank and they went to prostitutes in foreign countries. Be like us, the movie said. Griffith, because he's the star, got the girl, the daughter of a general, and rode his fast, cock-long, convertible car. He's like any good jock who would beat me up if they knew what I was thinking about their actor-king. In the end, Griffith is rewarded with a purple heart for being a good soldier. I heard that, after seeing this movie, some dumb guys went and signed up for the army. The army even placed recruitment tables outside the theaters. Little did these guys who signed up know but the army was not all pussy and fast cars. It was about death and cleaning the camp with a nice clean mop. My father was in the army during peacetime. He didn't see any action, just a lot of soapy water. Some of the worst years of his life, he said.

So Griffith's movie got people all mixed up and ready to kill. All his glamour looked so good and easy on screen, and made hard things seem palatable, but for those of us on the outside it only brought heartache. I watched that movie twice through and the rage kept building. It was a hot summer day, but I didn't have the fan on. I wanted my apartment as hot as possible so my body would cook with my mind. I saw Griffith's cute cadet face melting with the sweat.

I was drained after watching *A Kingdom of Trenches* but I wanted to push on. The more I watched, the more I knew I was right. The third movie I watched was called *On the House*. It was a small actor-piece about a restaurant in New York City. Not much can be said about this movie except that it was bad, pure talentless bad. Griffith always played the hero, the best teenager, the best soldier, the best waiter. But I found that I didn't even want to meet any of the characters he played. The waiter was so perfect and clean and boring I was almost tempted to turn it off halfway. I was glad I didn't. In the end his friend kills himself by slitting his wrists with shards of glass. There's blood all over the bathroom. Griffith discovers him in the bathtub and then screams, holding his friend in his arms, 'God help me,' in his best actor yell. Griffith's character deserved that kind of anguish and I was glad I hadn't turned it off before the end.

The next movie I watched was called *The March* about a hippie living in the sixties during the Vietnam War. The character was a poor hippie from a broken family. Most of the movie showed him at anti-war rallies and other hippie demonstrations. Now, this film made me as angry as *A Kingdom of Trenches*. For Griffith to make a movie with anti-war sentiments was just a lie. After *A Kingdom of Trenches* he shouldn't have ever been able to make a movie like that. Griffith was a fortune-paid hypocrite. He was lying to the world but he came off as passionate and people adored him. When I watched *Be All You Can Be*, another movie where he played a soldier, it nearly broke me. Griffith was pushing war on the world, making it glamorous and accessible, making it as pretty as his eyes. He was fooling everybody with his good-boy charm. But he was corrupt and hypocritical, playing pro-war here, anti-war there, rich man, poor man. He was as out of touch on screen as he was sitting in his beach home. And people believed in him. Man, was there something wrong.

The last movie I watched, called *Criminal Justice*, exemplified all those gold-chain yuppie ideals. He played a lawyer defending a man unjustly accused. He has his day in court and then drives off with his new pretty wife in a big, silver luxury car. The things that he was pushing on the world as being good and right were the things that were tearing the world apart. Quest for the rich world killed Marta and Sherry. And their death was killing me. People were dying. Maybe not physically, but their souls were. As I watched *Criminal Justice* I kept hoping he'd lose to the bad guy, get his face calmly bashed in, but of course he ends up winning, and he wins by pounding an old man, his former professor, into the ground.

I was fired and mad. I was about to write Griffith a second letter, pen in hand, when the phone rang.

'Hello?' I said.

'Ray Thompson?'

'Tompkins.'

'Oh, sorry. This is David, from upstairs.'

'David.'

'Yeah. I'm calling about the managerial position.'

'Uh-huh.'

'I've talked to the landlord and he said it would be all right if I gave the position to you.'

'Well, that's good,' I said.

'Yes. I'll drop off a list of the things you're supposed to do. I'm sure you can handle it.'

'I'm sure I can.'

I looked at the pen and the empty piece of typing paper, anxious.

'The only thing is, you won't be able to move into my apartment. It's already been filled by someone off the waiting list.'

'That's fine.'

'Good.'

'Hey, David?'

'Yeah?'

'How's your fucking movie coming along?'

He paused. Maybe he hadn't heard me right. 'It's going well. We go into production in another month.'

'Is Tim Griffith going to be in it?'

'It would be nice if he was, but I don't think so. Why?'

'Just wondering.'

'We may go with an unknown for the lead. I hope we don't but that's what they're saying.'

'David, that's just fucking great.'

'Well . . . uh . . . like I said, I'll drop off the papers you need. I'll leave my number if there are any problems.'

'OK.'

'OK?' he said, hesitantly, as if he thought he hadn't made the right decision.

'Right, the papers, bye.'

'Bye.'

This was better news than I let on. I hadn't planned on getting David's apartment so that wasn't a letdown. Having my 375 dollars a month rent paid would help a lot. I could work less at the parking garage and focus more of my attention on the new plans at hand.

As soon as I hung up with David, I was at my desk writing a second letter to Griffith.

Dear Mr Out-of-Touch,

I rented some of your movies today. I didn't realize until now how right I was about you. It's good to have some conviction. If you haven't guessed already, I'm the same person who delivered the other letter. I dropped it off myself. I saw your home. Why don't you feel some remorse living in all that wealth? Your beach house has three buildings while I'm confined to writing this from my small apartment. I'm surprised you can live with yourself.

You don't deserve all your fans and your money. Intelligent and moral men deserve praise, not men who are vacant and weak of mind. Not men who represent and justify simple thinking, smiling skin over ideas. But still you live on so stupid and guiltless.

I have this tendency to not get too close to people. Once more than two or three people start telling me that they like me and they want to be with me, I get out of their way. It gives me an uneasy feeling to be well-liked. But you. You have millions of people who love you for no good reason at all and you go on making movie after movie so more people will love you. Are you not man anymore, but pure ego? I ask you these questions because you should ask them of yourself. You're fucked, Griffith, and you are fucking other people.

All those young, mindless morons who signed up for the service after seeing 'A Kingdom of Trenches' have you to blame. You know how to ruin lives, Griffith.

You know as well as I that your movies aren't any good. They are hypocritical pieces of glossed-over trash. You know that you are getting away with murder. The public might laugh as you dance and fuck yourself on screen, but you fuck the public right back by making them cheer for the body over the mind, war over peace. You might look so cool and suave in the movies but you know it's only the editing that makes you look that way. You are nothing.

I'm telling you all this because this is a lesson you need, a *lesson of change. I have serious doubt that you are smart enough to make the transition from evil to innocent but there's still a chance. If you were smart you'd frame my letters, invite me to your house, and ask me for a lesson on how to run your life. Because if life is like school, you're failing. We could have a good relationship if only you'd realize that your Golden Calf values need to stop.*

I looked at your house with disgust. Your beach house is shaded by so many trees, to shelter you from so much bad feeling. But I am coming at you, regardless of how much comfort your money can buy. I will teach you and I will teach everybody if it kills you or me.

From,
Someone you're not going to get rid of

There was a knock at the door while I wrote. I didn't answer. David slid the managerial papers under the door. They just said that I had to make sure that everything with the electricity and plumbing was running smoothly and I had to collect everybody's rent at the end of the month. I was the halfway man between the tenants and the landlord. Just like I was the halfway man between the public and Tim Griffith.

Writing Griffith felt good, purposeful. I hadn't written or thought about anything so much in my life. I guessed bad feeling was a good catalyst. I felt like I was finally doing something positive with my life, after all the anger and slow boredom. I was still bitter but at least I was doing something about it, writing and thinking. For the first time I felt some sense of proud accomplishment.

I drove to the beach house to drop off the second letter. This time I wanted to do it quickly in case he had somebody on watch to catch me. I didn't put it beneath Griffith to hire guards for his palace gate. I drove over there in a rush, quick and excited. This was getting fun, like I was in one of Griffith's movies where the bad guy finally wins. One block before I hit Mountainview Terrace, I got out of the car and hung a shirt out of the trunk so it blocked the license plate. There wasn't a license plate on the front of the car. I got back into the car and drove right up to the mailbox, on the wrong side of the road so I could reach it from the driver's side. I gave a quick look around. No one seemed to be watching. I dropped the letter in the mailbox and drove away. I didn't waste any time.

Chapter Fifteen

HAPPIER THAN HELL

'RAY, THIS IS Bud Friedman from the college.'

'Hi, Bud.'

'I'm calling in regards to a student here.'

'What about a student?'

'I'm following up on some letters a student was sent. You wouldn't know anything about that would you?'

'How do you mean?'

'I'm wondering if you know anything about the letters.'

'What could I know about the letters?'

'I – I'm not insinuating anything, Ray. I just want to know if you have any information about the letters, maybe that you didn't tell us, or maybe that slipped your mind.'

'No.'

'The reason I'm asking is because she got another letter. And this one was bad, let me tell you, it was really sick. And this one was sent from the outside.'

'Where was the postmark?'

'Hollywood.'

'You know anybody who lives out there?'

'No. Not really. Some of the guys on the staff do, but I trust them, they've been here too long. I can't believe I've resorted to questioning them. I feel bad about it. It's just that the letters are so awful.'

'Huh.'

'Do you think you could give me a handwriting sample?'

'A handwriting sample?'

'Yeah, just to make sure. Most of the letters were typed but there was one written by hand. The other guys have agreed to do it.'

'But I didn't do anything.'

'I know, Ray.'

'Did she get any letters since I've been gone?'

'Yeah, she got one. That one was typed. And that was the bad one.'

'If I'm not there, why would I have any cause for sending letters?'

'I don't know. I suppose you're right.' He sighed. 'I'm sorry about this, Ray.'

'Don't worry about it.'

We were quiet for a couple of seconds. I imagined Bud crying. I imagined Helen crying. I imagined the whole college drowning in tears.

'Well, I . . . hope you catch the guy,' I said.

'So do I. Sorry to bother you.'

'I'll call you if I think of anything.'

'Thanks, do that.'

The phone call didn't bother me one bit. They would never catch me. That was part of the joy. Bud sounded desperate. He had no idea. Nobody did.

Before I moved on to Griffith, I wrote another letter to Helen. Just to keep her aware. It said:

Dear Helen,

Ha ha ha ha ha ha ha ha ha ha ha ha ha ha ha ha ha
ha ha ha ha ha ha ha ha ha ha ha ha ha ha ha ha ha ha ha
ha ha ha ha ha ha ha ha ha ha ha ha ha ha ha ha ha ha ha
ha ha ha ha ha ha ha ha ha ha ha ha ha ha ha ha ha ha ha
ha ha ha ha ha ha ha ha ha ha ha ha ha ha ha ha ha ha ha
ha ha ha ha ha ha ha ha ha ha ha ha ha ha ha ha ha ha ha
ha ha ha ha ha ha ha ha ha ha ha ha ha ha ha ha ha ha ha
ha ha ha ha ha ha ha ha ha ha ha ha ha ha ha ha ha ha ha

ha ha ha ha ha ha ha ha ha ha ha ha ha ha ha ha ha ha ha ha
ha ha ha ha ha ha ha ha ha ha ha ha ha ha ha ha ha ha ha ha
ha ha ha ha ha ha ha ha ha ha ha ha ha ha ha ha ha ha ha ha
ha ha ha ha ha ha ha ha ha ha ha ha ha ha ha ha ha ha ha ha
ha ha ha ha ha ha ha ha ha ha ha ha ha ha ha ha ha ha ha ha
ha ha ha ha ha ha ha ha ha ha ha ha ha ha ha ha ha ha ha ha
ha ha ha ha ha ha ha ha ha ha ha ha ha ha ha ha ha ha ha ha
ha ha ha ha ha ha ha ha ha ha ha ha ha ha ha ha ha ha ha ha
ha ha ha ha ha ha ha ha ha ha ha ha ha ha ha ha ha ha ha ha
ha ha ha ha ha ha ha ha ha ha ha ha ha ha ha ha ha ha ha ha
ha ha ha ha ha ha ha ha ha ha ha ha ha ha ha ha ha ha ha ha
ha ha ha ha ha ha ha ha ha ha ha ha ha ha ha ha ha ha ha ha
ha ha ha ha ha ha ha ha ha ha ha ha ha ha ha ha ha ha ha ha
ha ha ha ha ha ha ha ha ha ha ha ha ha ha ha ha ha ha ha ha
ha ha ha ha ha ha ha ha ha ha ha ha ha ha ha ha ha ha ha ha
ha ha ha ha ha ha ha ha ha ha ha ha ha ha ha ha ha ha ha ha
ha ha ha ha ha ha ha ha ha ha ha ha ha ha ha ha ha ha ha ha
ha ha ha ha ha ha ha ha ha ha ha ha ha ha ha ha ha ha ha ha
ha ha ha ha ha ha ha ha ha ha ha ha ha ha ha ha ha ha ha ha
ha ha ha ha ha ha ha ha ha ha ha ha ha ha ha ha ha ha ha ha
ha ha ha ha ha ha ha ha ha ha ha ha ha ha ha ha ha ha ha ha
ha ha ha ha ha ha ha ha ha ha ha ha ha ha ha ha ha ha ha ha
ha ha ha ha ha ha ha ha ha ha ha ha ha ha ha ha ha ha ha ha
ha ha ha ha ha ha ha ha ha ha ha ha ha ha ha ha ha ha ha ha
ha ha ha ha ha ha ha ha ha ha ha ha ha ha ha ha ha ha ha ha
ha ha ha ha ha ha ha ha ha ha ha ha ha ha ha ha ha ha ha ha
ha ha ha ha ha ha ha ha ha ha ha ha ha ha ha ha ha ha ha ha
ha ha ha ha ha ha ha ha ha ha ha ha ha ha ha ha ha ha ha ha
ha ha ha ha ha ha ha ha ha ha ha ha ha ha ha ha ha ha ha ha
ha ha ha ha ha ha ha ha ha ha ha ha ha ha ha ha ha ha ha ha
ha ha ha ha ha ha ha ha ha ha ha ha ha ha ha ha ha ha ha ha
ha ha ha ha ha ha ha ha ha ha ha ha ha ha ha ha ha ha ha ha
ha ha ha ha ha ha ha ha ha ha ha ha ha ha ha ha ha ha ha.

Ha ha ha ha ha ha ha ha ha ha ha ha ha ha ha ha ha ha
ha ha ha ha ha ha ha ha ha ha ha ha ha ha ha ha ha ha
ha ha ha ha ha ha ha ha ha ha ha ha ha ha ha ha ha ha
ha ha ha ha ha ha ha ha ha ha ha ha ha ha ha ha ha ha
ha ha ha ha ha ha ha ha ha ha ha ha ha ha ha ha ha ha
ha ha ha ha ha ha ha ha ha ha ha ha ha ha ha ha ha ha
ha ha ha ha ha ha ha ha ha ha ha ha ha ha ha ha ha ha
ha ha ha ha ha ha ha ha ha ha ha ha ha ha ha ha ha ha
ha ha ha ha ha ha ha ha ha ha ha ha ha ha ha ha ha ha
ha ha ha ha ha ha ha ha ha ha ha ha ha ha ha ha ha ha
ha ha ha ha ha ha ha ha ha ha ha ha ha ha ha ha ha ha
ha ha ha ha ha ha ha ha ha ha ha ha ha ha ha ha ha ha
ha ha ha ha ha ha ha ha ha ha ha ha ha ha ha ha ha ha
ha ha ha ha ha ha ha ha ha ha ha ha ha ha ha ha ha ha
ha ha ha ha ha ha ha ha ha ha ha ha ha ha ha ha ha ha
ha ha ha ha ha ha ha ha ha ha ha ha ha ha ha ha ha ha
ha ha ha ha ha ha ha ha ha ha ha ha ha ha ha ha ha ha
ha ha ha ha ha ha ha ha ha ha ha ha ha ha ha ha ha ha
ha ha ha ha ha ha ha ha ha ha ha ha ha ha ha ha ha ha
ha ha ha ha ha ha ha ha ha ha ha ha ha ha ha ha ha ha
ha ha ha ha ha ha ha ha ha ha ha ha ha ha ha ha ha ha
ha ha ha ha ha ha ha ha ha ha ha ha ha ha ha ha ha ha
ha ha ha ha ha ha ha ha ha ha ha ha ha ha ha ha ha ha
ha ha ha ha ha ha ha ha ha ha ha ha ha ha ha ha ha ha
ha ha ha ha ha ha ha ha ha ha ha ha ha ha ha ha ha ha
ha ha ha ha ha ha ha ha ha ha ha ha ha ha ha ha ha ha
ha ha ha ha ha ha ha ha ha ha ha ha ha ha ha ha ha ha
ha ha ha ha ha ha ha ha ha ha ha ha ha ha ha ha ha ha
ha ha ha ha ha ha ha ha ha ha ha ha ha ha ha ha ha ha
ha ha ha ha ha ha ha ha ha ha ha ha ha ha ha ha ha ha
ha ha ha ha ha ha ha ha ha ha ha ha ha ha ha ha ha ha
ha ha ha ha ha ha ha ha ha ha ha ha ha ha ha ha ha ha
ha ha ha ha ha ha ha ha ha ha ha ha ha ha ha ha ha ha
ha ha ha ha ha ha ha ha ha ha ha ha ha ha ha ha ha ha
ha ha ha ha ha ha ha ha ha ha ha ha ha ha ha ha ha ha
ha ha ha ha ha ha ha ha ha ha ha ha ha ha ha ha ha ha

ha ha ha ha ha ha ha ha ha ha ha ha ha ha ha ha ha
ha ha ha ha ha ha ha ha ha ha ha ha ha ha ha ha ha
ha ha ha ha ha ha ha ha ha ha ha ha ha ha ha ha ha
ha ha ha ha ha ha ha ha ha ha ha ha ha ha ha ha ha
ha ha ha ha ha ha ha ha ha ha ha ha ha ha ha ha ha
ha ha ha ha ha ha ha ha ha ha ha ha ha ha ha ha ha
ha ha ha ha ha ha ha ha ha ha ha ha ha ha ha ha ha
ha ha ha ha ha ha ha ha ha ha ha ha ha ha ha ha ha
ha ha ha ha ha ha ha ha ha ha ha ha ha ha ha ha ha
ha ha ha ha ha ha ha ha ha ha ha ha ha ha ha ha ha
ha ha ha ha ha ha ha ha ha ha ha ha ha ha ha ha ha
ha ha ha ha ha ha ha ha ha ha ha ha ha ha ha ha ha
ha ha ha ha ha ha ha ha ha ha ha ha ha ha ha ha ha
ha ha ha ha ha ha ha ha ha ha ha ha ha ha ha ha ha
ha ha ha ha ha ha ha ha ha ha ha ha ha ha ha ha ha
ha ha ha ha ha ha ha ha ha ha ha ha ha ha ha ha ha
ha ha ha ha ha ha ha ha ha ha ha ha ha ha ha ha ha
ha ha ha ha ha ha ha ha ha ha ha ha ha ha ha ha ha
ha ha ha ha ha ha ha ha ha ha ha ha ha ha ha ha ha
ha ha ha ha ha ha ha ha ha ha ha ha ha ha ha ha ha
ha ha ha ha ha ha ha ha ha ha ha ha ha ha ha ha ha
ha ha ha ha ha ha ha ha ha ha ha ha ha ha ha ha ha
ha ha ha ha ha ha ha ha ha ha ha ha ha ha ha ha ha
ha ha ha ha ha ha ha ha ha ha ha ha ha ha ha ha ha
ha ha ha ha ha ha ha ha ha ha ha ha ha ha ha ha ha
ha ha ha ha ha ha ha ha ha ha ha ha ha ha ha ha ha
ha ha ha ha ha ha ha ha ha ha ha ha ha ha ha ha ha
ha ha ha ha ha ha ha ha ha ha ha ha ha ha ha ha ha
ha ha ha ha ha ha ha ha ha ha ha ha ha ha ha ha ha
ha ha ha ha ha ha ha ha ha ha ha ha ha ha ha ha ha
ha ha ha ha ha ha ha ha ha ha ha ha ha ha ha ha ha
ha ha ha ha ha ha ha ha ha ha ha ha ha ha ha ha ha
ha ha ha ha ha ha ha ha ha ha ha ha ha ha ha ha ha
ha ha ha ha ha ha ha ha ha ha ha ha ha ha ha ha ha
ha ha ha.

*Ha ha ha ha ha ha ha ha ha ha ha ha ha ha ha ha ha ha
ha ha ha ha ha ha ha ha ha ha ha ha ha ha ha ha ha ha
ha ha ha ha ha ha ha ha ha ha ha ha ha ha ha ha ha ha
ha ha ha ha ha ha ha ha ha ha ha ha ha ha ha ha ha ha
ha ha ha ha ha ha ha ha ha ha ha ha ha ha ha ha ha ha
ha ha ha ha ha ha ha ha ha ha ha ha ha ha ha ha ha ha
ha ha ha ha ha ha ha ha ha ha ha ha ha ha ha ha ha ha
ha ha ha ha ha ha ha ha ha ha ha ha ha ha ha ha ha ha
ha ha ha ha ha ha ha ha ha ha ha ha ha ha ha ha ha ha
ha ha ha ha ha ha ha ha ha ha ha ha ha ha ha ha ha ha
ha ha ha ha ha ha ha ha ha ha ha ha ha ha ha ha ha ha
ha ha ha ha ha ha ha ha ha ha ha ha ha ha ha ha ha ha
ha ha ha ha ha ha ha ha ha ha ha ha ha ha ha ha ha ha
ha ha ha ha ha ha ha ha ha ha ha ha ha ha ha ha ha ha
ha ha ha ha ha ha ha ha ha ha ha ha ha ha ha ha ha.*

Love Me

I was laughing the whole time I wrote them down. I could have
written that letter for the rest of my life. It came straight from
the heart. Lovely Helen.

I rented three new Griffith movies. One movie called *The Stone*
set in medieval times. It was pretty to look at but that had nothing
to do with Griffith, it was just a pretty movie. Another called *The
Winning Team* about football, instilling more of that jock ethic.
And finally, one called *Distant Calls* set in turn-of-the-century
England where he had an English accent and starred with his
wife, but I didn't even make it a half hour before I had to shut
it off because it was so bad. I was getting madder and madder.

I had hoped that there was a Griffith movie that I could see
in the theater. I checked the paper. There wasn't one. There
wasn't even one in the theaters that showed late-run movies for
cheap. There was one movie starring his wife, Robin Culver.
Lately she had been branching out and starring in movies of
her own. The movie was called *Till Death Do Us Part*. There

was only one review in the ad, by a Dallas reviewer, that said, 'Mordantly funny.'

Luckily, the movie was playing in Santa Monica, close to my Venice home. It was playing at a four-dollar theater. I guessed it wasn't that important a movie.

There was a show in ten minutes. I was hoping to walk but that would take me at least thirty minutes. So I drove. I found the theater and struggled to find parking. I drove around and around the block, watching people steadily go inside the theater as I passed. The theater was next to a residential neighborhood so there were 'No Parking' signs everywhere. There were several long, empty spaces with the red and white signs. I was frustrated because the movie was going to start any minute.

Eventually I gave in and parked in an illegal space. It was too good to pass up, only half a block from the theater. The red 'No' hung in judgment over my car.

I missed the previews and most of the credits. I walked down the dark aisle as it said on screen, 'Directed by Daniel De Haven,' in front of an image of a Southern mansion with pillars and moss hanging off the roof. As the credits faded away, Robin Culver walked out of the house, hair dyed blond, wearing a bikini.

The movie was a strange comedy about a Southern family who are all inbred. Cousins sleeping with sisters talking in thick Southern accents. It was supposed to be funny, but I couldn't follow it because I couldn't tell what was supposed to be funny and what was supposed to be serious. The mood was in the music, jumpy music played with high-pitched horns. The funny music even played in the end, when there was a murder. It was a funny murder.

I wanted to dislike Culver but I just couldn't. She was a decent actress. She used subtle facial expressions. She didn't overdo it like some of the other actors in the movie. She expressed a calm confidence. She was a better actor than her husband. I was really looking to hate her too, but I just couldn't find it in myself.

What was unsettling about her was the way she looked. She

was pretty in a great, exaggerated way. An alien, effortless beauty. Almost too pretty, rigid. There wasn't a flaw on her body. And throughout the movie she wore these high-cut mini-skirts. Long, thin, tan legs. She didn't have a scratch. Her eyes were perfectly aligned and a glassy sea-blue. Her nose was chiseled and came to a point. She must have made some women silently scream to themselves.

The movie, and even Culver, wasn't really important. What was important was the experience of being in a movie theater. I hadn't been to a movie in a while and I had forgotten what it was like. It was a strange scene, a movie theater. There was something creepy and intimate about sitting in a room and watching a movie with a crowd of people.

Going to the theater that day was good for me. The movie might not have been very good but I got a new feeling for how movies worked. The music swelled with those loudspeakers, the big screen overwhelmed your senses and it all went straight to the heart. It was much different than renting a movie. A movie on TV didn't quite have that same immediacy as it did in the theater. Renting a movie was like listening to a sermon on a tape recorder instead of in church, without the loud echo and stained glass. The movie theater was Griffith's pulpit. The swelling music with the special stereo sound backed up his bad morals and his button nose.

I seemed to be the only one who gave this any thought because when I looked around all I saw were hypnotized faces looking up at the screen and the screen alone, most of their fingers wet with butter.

There were some things in this life that were very, very strange if you stopped and thought about it. Going to the movies like some crazy cathedral was one of them. Parking signs were another. Eating was too. Eating and shitting. Yeah, sometimes it felt damn weird to be human.

When I got outside, there were two parking tickets tucked on either side of my windshield. They were both for fifty dollars.

I wasn't surprised. I wasn't surprised by much of anything anymore.

From there, my plan was to drive to a magazine stand I knew about. The stand was almost as long as a city block. It even kept some of the foreign papers. I was hoping to find an article about Griffith in one of the entertainment magazines. I was out of luck. There weren't any. I searched five magazines. It seemed like he was everywhere all the time but that day I couldn't even find a picture of him. I figured I would have to get back issues at my local library branch. I drove home to get my library card.

I was on my way out the door to the library when I got a phone call. I tripped over my pant cuffs which had fallen below my shoes. I picked up the phone on my knees.

'Hello?' I said.

'Ray, it's your mother.'

'My mother?'

'Yes.'

'What is it?' I said, very aggravated.

'Will you please come visit me?'

'No.' I almost hung up on her.

'Please?'

'Why?'

'You haven't been here in so long.'

'I was there for Christmas.'

'That's different. I want you to visit now. Besides, Christmas was months ago.'

'I don't have the time.'

'You can make time, I'm sure.'

Her voice was sad and pleading. Sadder and more pleading than usual.

'Are you dating anyone now?' I asked.

'Oh, Ray, that's my question,' she said nervously.

'Are you?'

'No, Ray, I'm not.'

'So now you need my company.'

'That's not it. Oh, Ray, just please come over.' She sounded desperate that time.

'Why? What is it?'

'Your dad. He's been coming around again.'

'He has? What's he been doing?'

'He's just been standing outside the house sometimes at night, just looking at the windows. I peeked through the curtains. I'm worried, Ray.'

'It's been a while since he's done that, huh?'

'Yes, it's been years. I really thought he'd gotten over that.'

'He's harmless. I wouldn't worry.'

'Well, you know last time he came into the house and he . . .'

'And he what?' I asked. But I knew. I knew exactly what he did. He raped her. She didn't know I knew. She didn't know he called me afterwards, that very night, and with crank-call heavy breathing told me all about it, every detail. I slept for four days straight after that phone call, playing sick to the warehouse.

'And he – oh, never mind,' she said. 'Will you just come and stay with me for a little while?'

'Well, Mom, I've just got this job as apartment manager and I really can't leave.'

'Raymond!' she yelled. That was a command.

'OK, Mom, I'll come over and see what Dad wants. But I can't stay for long. I have some business that I have to take care of.'

'That's fine. Please come.'

'All right. I'll be over some time today.'

'Good.' She paused. I could hear her anxious breathing. 'Raymond?'

'What?'

'You got a job as apartment manager?'

'Yes.'

'I'm glad,' she said.

'OK, Mom, I'll see you.'

I packed a bag so I could stay a couple of nights. On my way over to the house I stopped at the library to find old magazines on Griffith.

I told the woman at the periodicals desk that I needed articles on Griffith. She was a pretty lady. Thin, average height, with little librarian glasses. She gave me a friendly look. I gave her one back. 'The computer is over there,' she pointed. 'Just type in the subject and it will show you a list of periodicals.'

I must have looked dumbfounded because she smiled and said, 'I'll help you.'

She walked me to the computer and tenderly started typing. 'Tim Griffith, you said?'

'Yes, Tim Griffith. Alias "scumbag."'

Her warm smile turned to a frown and she said, 'I'm sure you can take it from here.' She walked away with a bad glance over her shoulder, no longer the friendly, flirting librarian.

'Fuck it,' I thought.

I chose four different articles on Griffith. One was about him and his wife, one was a cover story from *Entertainment Weekly*, one was a big article in *GQ*, and the last was an article, new that week, about his new movie in *Variety*.

I wrote down the call numbers and brought them to the counter where the pretty librarian was standing and she got my articles like a frowning robot.

I read all four articles straight through right there in the library. They reinforced all my convictions. He was even more fake than I'd already thought. He changed his name from Richard Gruson to something more safe and glamorous. He was deep into environmental causes and the New Age bullshit religion called Scientology. He probably thought the environmental causes balanced out all of his wealth. But the environment was a rich man's cause. He could go to rallies and not worry about offending anyone. Everyone liked green trees. In the *Entertainment Weekly* article it said that Griffith went on far-away retreats to meditate with other celebrities. They all wanted to be even further removed from real life than they already were. They thought they could touch God. It wasn't enough that their movies were a fantasy, their lives had to be a fantasy as well. They lived in pure luxury. Griffith was their leader. The article made it seem like nothing in the world existed but him. Like if you weren't there praying and screaming about the environment, or lounging by his wide, peanut-shaped pool, where he lay wearing sunglasses and a grin, then you were nobody. Towards the end, the article said, 'Tim Griffith sometimes loses himself in *Dianetics*. "The book keeps my mind and my goals in focus," says the actor. Lately, Scientology has garnered a large following among actors and others in Hollywood.' Griffith was brainwashed and he was brainwashing the people into following all his dark causes. For the *GQ* article he posed like a model, the different brands of clothes written in the corner, like 'Suit by Armani 1500 dollars.'

I xeroxed all the articles so I could read them again at my leisure. I especially wanted to keep the *Variety* article because it had information about where his new movie was being filmed.

With cold thoughts on my mind, I drove to my mom's.

My mom's place looked different than it did when I was growing up. She did little things to the house to make it look less like where a family lived and more where a single woman, who had a life of her own, lived. She took the family pictures off the walls, certainly the ones of my father, but even the pictures of me. There was one, the size of a silver dollar, in an oval frame on her dresser. She bought a big, cheap, imitation Persian rug. The rug looked immediately fake because it had colors of hot pink and lime green. She laid that down in the living room over the tan wall-to-wall carpeting, under the same chipped brown coffee table I'd grown up with. She also bought some flea-market paintings that my father would have never let her keep. The one over the mantel was of three blurred figures who were twisting and turning inside one another and if you stared at it long enough it looked like they were fucking. The painting that used to be there was of a moosehead on a wall. My father thought that was so funny. You see, it was a *painting* of a moosehead and not an actual moosehead. What a funny man. The other painting was a purely sentimental portrait of a lake, which hung over the dining room table. My father would have called that 'girl-crap.' There were countless other things all over the place, little porcelain elephants, flowerless vases. She had gotten them just to prove that she had a mind of her own, like a kid who's left home for the first time. I could bet on there being something new when I got there.

She opened the door quickly. She held her finger in the air, said, "One minute," and rushed to her bedroom. Her bedroom was now yellow instead of white. There was a queen-sized bed instead of a double. She was on the phone.

I sat on my childhood living room couch and stared at the painting of the people fucking. My mom was talking animatedly in the other room but I couldn't make out the words, just the emotion. The emotion of a flirting little girl. When she came out she didn't look so lively. She looked tired and maybe a little sad. Withered was how she looked.

She tried to brighten her eyes and smile. 'Hi, Ray, you've lost weight,' she said. 'That's the first thing I thought when I saw you. I noticed it right away.'

'That's nice, Mom. Not how nice it is to see your son, but that he looks thin.'

'That's not what I meant. You really have lost weight.'

'You look about the same.'

'Well . . . thank you.' She looked confused, as if she thought I'd insulted her.

'Would you like a drink?' she asked.

'Sure.'

She went into the kitchen. She came back with two Scotches on ice, hers in a tall glass, mine wide and short. She hadn't asked me what I wanted.

'Hey, Mom, have you ever noticed that if you stare at

that painting long enough it looks like all of them are fucking?'

She paused and frowned. 'Yes, Ray, you've mentioned that.'

Another pause. 'So who was that on the phone?' I asked.

'Oh, an acquaintance.'

'An acquaintance? Do you mean a boyfriend? Are you going
out with him, this acquaintance?'

'Please, Ray.' She took a sip and changed the subject. 'You
know what I want to do? I'd love to go to the La Brea Tar Pits.
Sometimes it just helps me to relax.'

'The tar pits, huh?'

'Well, not the tar pits, but the park they have around them.
They have a lovely park near the tar pits.'

I didn't want to go but I said OK. I felt better outside the
house. When I was inside I felt like another man she brought
home. Drinking Scotch and waiting to go into the bedroom.

I drove because she said she didn't like to drive anymore. 'The
streets are just too crowded now,' she said. I knew the real reason
was because her eyes were getting bad and she was too proud to
wear glasses.

We walked through the park, basically just a large lawn and,
for the most part, treeless. The smell of tar hung thick in the air.
In some parts of the lawn, the grass was muddied by tar that had
seeped through the earth. I couldn't see why she liked it there.

'I don't know what to do about Jerry,' she said.

'I'll talk to him,' I said.

'It's just that he hasn't really seen anyone since, you know, the
divorce. He must get so lonely.' She said this a little proudly, as
if his solitude were a victory.

'He's doing fine.'

'I know Jerry. He's not a bad looking man. He can find a nice
lady.' Jesus, listen to her, I thought. That patronizing way we
knew so well.

'It's not as easy as you think,' I said. 'Just give him a few
days. He'll be fine.'

She stepped over a patch of moist, black grass. I let my feet sink in. Moisture came through my broken shoes. I felt the wetness between my toes. It was uncomfortable, but also comfortable in a way. It felt deviant.

'Anyway, what have you been doing?' she said.

'Nothing much.'

'How's your job?'

'Which job?'

'The job as security guard.'

'I don't have that job anymore,' I said and looked to the sky. It was a thick blue, as if painted.

'You don't? Then what do you do?' Shock in her voice.

'I'm doing fine. The manager job pays my rent.'

'But what do you do for food?'

'I work in a parking garage sometimes.' She gave me a cold, sour look. If rotten milk had eyes. 'But that's OK because I'm doing other things,' I said.

'Like what?'

'That doesn't matter.'

'It's so hard to keep track of all your jobs.' She sighed. 'Are you seeing anyone?'

'Jesus, do we have to have the same conversation every time we see each other?'

'Don't yell at me. I just want to know some things about you.'

'Well, now you know them. Ask me something else.'

She stopped to think of something else but she couldn't do it. She opened her mouth to say something but then stopped herself.

'Jesus, you're pathetic.'

'Now, c'mon, Ray.' She tried to smile.

We were walking towards the tar pits. Tourists were standing around snapping pictures of the woolly mammoth family that was being sucked under the tar. The young mammoth yelled to its mother. The mother threw its head in the air, crying out in pain and fear, sinking into the tar. The tourists' kids, all white, were running around, ice-cream stained and frantic.

'Do you want to go into the museum?' she asked me.

'No, I can see Neanderthals right here in the park.'

'What?'

Right then, a kid of about six carrying an ice-cream cone came running towards us. He was running so fast that the ice cream fell in a ball off the cone and landed on the cement. He was so startled that he fell himself. The boy picked up the ball of chocolate and started crying, the chocolate melting through his fingers. He sat there in front of us, the ice cream dripping on his legs. I couldn't help but laugh. It was such a pathetic, stupid scene. Made by incompetence. My laugh grew and grew. The mom came running up and she picked up her kid and stared at me laughing. The ice cream fell again from his hand. The kid cried louder. The mom gave me a hateful glare as I wiped the tears from my eyes.

'Ray, how can you be so insensitive?'

I was still laughing.

My mom looked worried. My laughing calmed down.

But then I stared at the ball of chocolate lying alone on the pavement, slowly melting, and I started laughing again. I laughed hard and deep, making it difficult to breathe. I almost wished it would stop. It was painful and I was afraid that if I laughed so hard I might rupture an organ. But the laughs kept coming.

The mom and kid were gone and the ice cream just lay there, alone on the pavement. The kid went away holding only a cone, ice cream all over his hand. I couldn't stand it. Every time I looked at the melted ball of ice cream I started laughing again. I had to get out of there or the laughter would never stop. I concentrated hard on the mammoth family sinking in the tar and finally they died down.

My mom didn't say anything more about it and neither did I. We didn't say much to each other except 'Where did we park the car?' and 'Do you have my keys?' until later that night. On the drive home I thought about the scene, that goddamn ball of chocolate melting on the pavement, and I began laughing again. I had to pull over and have her drive, my eyes were so full of tears.

Chapter Sixteen

DAD

THAT NIGHT MY mom made Chicken Parmesan and I was grateful. I hadn't eaten well for a long time. I had been eating soup from a can and the occasional pasta with sauce from a jar. I probably *was* getting thinner.

She didn't mention the park. She probably blocked it out. Throughout my childhood she would forget bad times like they never happened. That was another way we were different. I never let myself forget bad times. We talked about mom–son trivialities until nine o'clock when she said, 'Jerry came over about this time last night,' and she peered out the window. 'He's not there now.'

'Maybe he won't show. Maybe he's gotten over it.'

'I don't know.'

She kept looking out the window every five minutes.

'If you didn't keep looking out the window you wouldn't know he was there and it wouldn't be a problem.'

'Yes, but I want you to talk to him,' she said, peering behind the curtain. 'I'm afraid he'll do something.'

'Just relax.'

At 9.45 she spotted him. 'There he is,' she said. 'Come look.' She almost seemed excited.

I walked over to the window.

'Don't open the curtain too wide,' she said. 'Make sure he doesn't see you.'

I looked outside. There was my father. I hadn't seen him in close to a year. I didn't go over to his place for the holidays.

He told me he was going to Mexico with a friend. I didn't know whether or not to believe him. I wasn't sure if he had any friends.

He was standing in the street, his feet touching the curb. So he wasn't trespassing the property. He was wearing tan slacks and a light-blue button-down shirt, his work clothes at the shoe repair shop. He was also wearing a heavy tan jacket. He must have been hot because it was a ninety-degree night.

'Do you see him?' my mother said.

'Yeah, I see him.'

'What do you think he wants?'

'I don't know. How should I know?'

'He just stands there like that. It's creepy.'

I watched him. Watched him watching. He didn't move.

'Well, what now?' I said.

'Maybe you should go out and talk to him.'

'You sure you want me to do that?'

'I don't know what I want.'

'I could just stay here tonight in case he comes in.'

'But what if he comes back when you're not here?'

'I don't know,' I said.

'Please talk to him. I think you better.'

I wasn't any less afraid of my father than she was. I peered out the curtain again. He had put his hands in his pockets.

My mom pushed me towards the door. The door closed and I was alone outside. I looked at my father, feeling like I had to talk a person away from suicide. I didn't want to be here, a mediator between two evils. I didn't feel the heat in the air. I got the shivers.

'Hello, Ray,' said my father.

I moved towards him. He stayed where he was.

'Are you here to help Janice?'

For a second I thought, 'Who's Janice?' but then I remembered that was the pet name he had for my mom. Her name was Janet but for the first month they knew each other he thought her name was Janice. So the name stuck.

'How have you been?' he asked.

'I've been fine.'

'What have you been doing with yourself?'

'Not too much.'

'Saving your mother from the lurkings of strange men,' he said with no emotion, a smoker's voice.

'She says you've been coming around.'

'I can't lie. I have been.'

'She's been worried so she called me.'

'She's been worried, huh?'

'Yeah.'

'I have to tell you something about your mother, Ray.' He stopped. He didn't tell me anything.

'What?'

His eyes went to his feet. 'Your mother's a whore,' he said.

I looked back at the house. I could see my mom peering from behind the curtain in the dining room. He had probably been able to see her peering all this time.

'Did you hear me?' he said.

'Yeah.'

'I think you know what I'm talking about.'

'That doesn't mean you should come around here like this.'

'I've seen her. She goes out with a different guy every night of the week.'

'I don't know, Jerr—'

'What, you're going to call me Jerry? I'm your father. Call me Dad.'

'Fine, Dad.'

My mom walked out of the house then. I didn't know why she did. She walked along the cracked cement walkway and stood by the garage. We were standing in a triangle, me on the lawn, Dad in the street, and her in the driveway.

'Hello, Jerry,' she said.

'Janice.'

'My name is Janet. Call me Janet.'

My dad mumbled something I couldn't hear.

'Why are you coming around the house?' she said.

'Mom, I thought I was going to deal with this.'

'I can stand up for myself,' she said with shaky pride.

'Jesus.'

'I really wish you'd stop coming around.'

'Why do you go out with a different man every night of the week?' he said, a little desperately. Jerry, my father.

'That's no concern of yours.'

'That's certainly a concern of mine. It's a concern what my ex-wife is doing.'

'I'm just trying to make a life for myself, Jerry.'

'Fucking different men, that what you call a life?'

'C'mon, Dad.'

He looked at me, then to her, then back at me again.

'You're mother's a whore, Ray. Janice – I mean Janet – you're a whore.'

She didn't say anything. Nobody did.

Then he moved a few steps on to the driveway, closer to her. 'A whore goes out with a different man every night.'

She pulled back and winced as if he'd hit her. She started biting her red-painted nails.

'I'm just trying to enjoy myself. You should do the same. You should try going out sometimes,' she said.

'Oh shit, Janet, I should. I don't know if I have any judgment anymore. I mean, I married a whore.'

'Jerry,' I said. 'Why don't you go home. I'll come over to see you tomorrow.'

'What do you know, you're a whore's son.'

He bent down and picked up a loose brick from the flowerbed. He held it in his hand and studied it like he was trying to gauge its weight.

'Jesus, Dad.'

'Jesus,' he said.

He held the brick high above him like he was going to throw it at my mom and I took a step towards him to stop him. But, with a sad glance, he turned and threw it at a car. The brick went through the back windshield. It didn't make much of a sound, just a loud thump. The car wasn't mine or my mom's or his, it was a stranger's car. There was a round hole in the center of the windshield.

'I'll see you, Ray,' he said. He walked away, quickly, as if he didn't want to get caught. He started up his car, an old brown Nova, and peered at us as he drove away with the headlights off.

My mother and I looked at each other briefly and we walked back inside the house.

The front door closed behind us. She locked the deadbolt and said, 'Thank you.'

I didn't reply.

'I fixed your bed. You can sleep in your bedroom.'

'Fine, thanks,' I said and we went to our separate beds.

I fell asleep immediately and dreamt of childhood. Making a snowman, carrot and all, in the park by our house, an unreal, innocent time when there was pretty snowfall in LA. It was a decent dream.

My bedroom had been turned into a second den. There was a rocking chair, footstool, shelves of cookbooks and bestsellers, a small black and white TV, and the bed where I slept. My mom didn't use the room much but now it didn't look like a room where a kid lived, with football posters and that bad little kid smell. There was nothing in there to remind her that she was a mother.

At noon my mom woke me up and told me she'd made pancakes. She was at the table in a light-blue robe. I sat down and ate. The pancakes were eggy, like bad coffee-shop pancakes. She ate only one herself and we sat in silence.

'Do you want some more? There's more.'

'Sure.'

She went into the kitchen and brought out another stack. She looked sad in that robe, hair undone, shiny circles under her eyes.

'Are we not going to talk about last night?' I said.

'It will work itself out.' She looked at me blankly.

'Yeah?'

'Yes. Remember when you were a boy and you'd lose something. I would tell you that it would turn up. And it always did. Things always have a way of healing themselves.'

'Right, ignore it.'

She sighed. 'Ray, why do you always have to be so negative?'

I stopped eating and looked at her.

'You're always so harsh.'

'That's just my way.' I went back to eating, heavy butter, heavy syrup.

'You'll never get anywhere in this world if that's your way.'

'No?'

'No. People like friendliness.' She smiled as if to show friendliness.

'You expect me to be friendly after what happened last night?'

She answered as if she hadn't heard me. 'You'll never go anywhere if you don't smile.'

'Just smile away even if things aren't any good?'

'Yes.' She looked confused, as if I'd cornered her. She straightened the butter and the syrup bottle so that the labels faced her.

'I guess I'm not going to go anywhere then,' I said.

'Oh, Ray, don't you want to do something with yourself?'

'I am doing things.'

'Something more than that parking garage.'

'I have been doing things lately.'

'Like what?'

'I can't tell you.'

'Why not?'

'Because you're not ready to know about it,' I said.

'What do you mean?'

'They're important things. Soon I am going to be involved in something very important and you'll know what I'm talking about. I finally found satisfying work.'

'I don't understand. I don't understand you, Ray.'

'You will. Everybody will.'

'Fine. But I still think you should get a different job.'

I shoved away from the table and went over to the living room couch. I left my second stack of pancakes unfinished. They weren't very good. I sat down and watched her finish her one pancake in silence. I was getting antsy to write another letter. I could feel my veins pumping blood to my hands, telling them to pick up a pen and write. I thought this must be what it felt like to be an artist, eager to get back to the canvas. As though, if I didn't pick up a brush, I would feel like half a person. It was a welcome kind of pain.

I started leafing through a pile of magazines on the coffee table. At the bottom of the pile there was a magazine with an article about Griffith. It said in white letters in the corner of the cover, 'Tim Griffith tells about life, love, and his new movie.'

'Where did you get this?' I asked.

She looked over from clearing plates. 'I don't know. The dentist's, maybe.'

I flipped right to the section about Griffith, page 136. It was an interview. My heart started beating faster. I hadn't read an entire interview with him yet.

There was one picture of him, a full page portrait. He was smiling smugly with his hand under his chin. He was wearing a white shirt with the sleeves rolled back, dark black jeans and black shoes which shined in the photographer's light.

The interviewer asked him about rumors of divorce but he denied it. 'I love Robin. I always will. We are perfect for each other.' She asked him what direction he thought his career was going. He said: 'I'm very happy with the way things are going right now. I want to make movies that are strong and entertaining, but responsible in the sense that they give a good social message.'

She asked: 'Do you think you'll make another movie with your wife, Robin Culver?'

'We have no plans, but the last one was such a good experience that we may do it again. In some ways that kind of close-knit work situation can be hard on a relationship, but with us I think it made our marriage stronger.'

'And what about kids?'

'Robin's three months pregnant so she won't be working seriously for some time. We're concentrating on the family. I'm looking forward to it. My father was in banking and he traveled a lot. I don't want to be like that with my child. I don't want to be an absentee parent. But it's going to be hard because we're so busy.'

'Your last marriage broke up. How are you going about this marriage differently?'

'Well, I think that some people are more compatible than others. After a few years of marriage you learn things about each other, essentially if you are compatible. You learn if you get along well with each other. It's a slow process. Sometimes it works, sometimes it doesn't.'

'So you're staying with Robin Culver?'

He laughed. 'Yes, of course. We're happy. I'm happier than I've been in all my life. You know, yesterday at home I was looking at Robin and I just felt lucky. I can't forget how fortunate I really am.'

The interviewer wrote that Griffith looked like a man in love. 'Giddy as a first love,' it said.

I set down the magazine. My eyes were wide. I'll show Griffith, I thought. I'd been too easy on him up to this point. Teaching wasn't all he needed. He needed something hard, something coarse, something brutal that would knock him into shape. He needed punishment. No one should ride so high. It wasn't fair.

I stared at the painting of the three bodies fucking. I could see them moving. Their bodies were moving back and forth and sweating like Sherry and Don Gold.

I threw down the magazine and felt myself about to cry. All I could think was, goddammit, giddy as a first love. My parents were first loves. What did he know about that?

I went back to my room so I could pack my things and leave. My mom begged me to stay. 'Could you just stay another night?' she said.

'I've got work to do,' I told her.

'You can do it here,' she said.

That was true. All I needed was a pen and paper and she had that. I agreed to stay over and that night I sat in a wooden rocking chair in my old, childless room and wrote another letter.

Chapter Seventeen

DEVIL'S ADVOCATE

'WHAT ARE YOU writing?' asked my mom.

'Nothing,' I replied. 'Just something that will change the world,' I thought.

'Well, come on out soon, I want some company.'

I didn't answer and kept writing.

Dear Griffith,

You say that you are 'fortunate' but what fortune is there in being morally and ethically disfigured? You are a moral failure, Griffith. Usually failure is a good teacher but you just keep getting worse. I am going to make you feel the curse of your contentment.

I watched your wife naked through the beach-house window. She has a good body even when she's pregnant. You don't know what I'd like to do to your family. I don't think I'll tell you what I'm going to do. I think I'll keep it a secret and let you live in fear. How is it to fuck your wife? I'd very much like to know. Can you feel the baby kicking at your stomach when you're on top of her?

I am going to throw a brick in your life, Griffith. I will show the world what a false man you are. I will make you suffer like the rest of us. I am going to ruin you. Afterwards, you will be a broken man. That will be your real lesson. I will teach you like a ruler on the back of the hand. And then my job will be done.

I will show the world that you are nothing. That you are

subject to frailty. And then your whole backwards glamour
world won't seem as appealing. Just you wait. Just you wait.
  That's all I'm going to tell you now. I want you to live in
terrible fear.

I liked that letter. Especially the part about him being disfigured.
I joined my mother for drinks in the living room.

I drove to Mountainview as usual. I didn't yet know what I
had planned for Griffith. For now, I wanted him to live in fear
like I said. The fear and uncertainty were probably worse than
anything.

Everyone lived their life in waiting, uncertain and unfulfilled.
Most times, in the end, there was only pain and disappointment.
Griffith was going to have the same. He would live like most
people. Like his adoring goddamn public.

I put the sweatshirt over the license plate and drove up to the
mailbox. I dropped the letter in. As soon as I did, a long black
car which was parked in front of the house drove toward me and
stopped in front of my car so that our headlights were staring
at each other. The door on the driver's side opened and a man
wearing a gray suit without a tie started to get out. He shut the
door slowly, almost politely. Before he could look at me, I put the
car in reverse. I pressed my foot to the floor and drove full speed
backwards up Mountainview. I almost hit a row of flowerpots and
the Neighborhood Watch sign. The man got back into his car and
drove after me. I turned the car around in a quick three-point turn
in the middle of the street and drove fast into the PCH traffic.
Keeping my eye in the rear-view mirror, I drove down PCH.
I saw him around ten cars behind me. I sped up and weaved
around some more cars. He was far back. There was a stoplight
ahead. I took a left on to Malibu Road and parked on the dirt side
of the road when I saw that he didn't follow me. I checked and
checked the rear-view mirror. I didn't know if I should get out of
the car and hide or drive further up the hill. I sat in the car thirty

minutes watching the small rectangular movie of cars going by. He didn't come up the road. I drove home, pounding nervous. I almost felt stage fright, as if I'd fucked up the scene in front of an audience. Or like a kid giving a scared oral report in front of all the world.

At least I dropped off the letter.

I had a lot of ideas about what I should do to Griffith. He needed to pay for sicking a suit in a government car on me like a dog. I needed to leave a real message. Not just another letter. Something that he couldn't get away from. Something that put me more in control. I decided to break into his Bel-Air home. He wasn't there and I had a feeling that he didn't know that I knew about that house. I never said anything about the Bel-Air home in any of my letters.

On the way over there I stopped off at the market to get one of those sweet Jack Daniels coolers. They had become my favorite drink. They were easy to swallow and got you just as drunk.

I parked a block away from the Bel-Air house like I had the last time. I looked around but there didn't seem to be any black car waiting for me. I walked along the outer gate and looked for a way in. There didn't seem to be one. The wall was too high to climb over. On the right of the house there was a thick, solid bush, twenty feet high. The house on that side also had a tall black front gate.

There was an eight-foot brick wall in front of the house on the left of Griffith's. I couldn't get over it. Even if I did I wouldn't have been to able to get over the black gate separating the side of the house. Also I couldn't afford to take too much time without someone noticing me.

I tried as hard as I could to find a way in but I couldn't. I sat on the curb across from the house and wondered.

I was standing in front of the house, studying it hard like a contractor studies land, when somebody walked out of the house. I was about to run to the car when I saw that it was just a young Spanish woman. She hadn't even seen me. She was walking towards the gate. She stopped at the gate and turned a key. The gate opened wide enough for one person to get through. She walked through, turned the key again in a lock next to the doorbell, and the gate slowly closed.

She hadn't seen me yet.

When she saw me, she jumped back a little. 'Oh, hello,' she said with a slight accent.

'Hello.'

'Are you a fan?' she said.

Pause. 'Yes.'

'We get fans coming around here a lot.'

'I imagine.'

'I don't know how they all get the address.'

She stood there for a moment, smiling slightly, and she wasn't making a motion to leave, as if she liked talking to people who came around the house. She was small and cute up close. She was wearing tight acid-wash jeans. Her hair was long and soft and she had smooth dark skin. I had a thing for Spanish ladies. Sometimes I'd watch the Spanish TV station. I couldn't understand a word but I liked the Spanish ladies.

She looked me up and down, almost sexily. 'He's not here right now,' she said.

'I know. What do you do here?'

'I'm the maid. I'm one of the maids.'

'Would you like to get something to eat?' I asked her.

'No, I can't,' she said. 'I have a boyfriend.'

'You don't have a boyfriend. I can tell, you're lying.'

She smiled. 'You're perceptive.'

'Maybe. I can tell a liar.'

'I have to get home now,' she said and turned to walk down the street.

'What days do you work?' I asked.

She smiled softly and sweetly. 'I have to go.'

She walked away and left me standing there watching her. She was walking the half-mile to Sunset where she was probably going to catch the bus that would take her deep into downtown LA, just like all the Mexican maids. Maybe she was illegal. It was just like Griffith to have a pretty, cheaply-paid maid.

As I watched her walk down the black paved street, I realized that she was the closest thing I had to being inside the house. If I could become friendly enough with her, maybe she would invite me inside. I had to do something. Something to show Griffith that I was smarter than him, that I was a man of consequence, and that he wasn't as good as he seemed. Something to fulfill everything I'd written in the letters. God, I had dreams. Maybe I could get into his bedroom. This Spanish maid was like a key.

Right now, I had given up on breaking into the Bel-Air home. I looked at the lock that opened the gate but those kind of locks were impossible to pick. It was the same kind of circular lock that opened a vending machine. I was lost. I could barely pick a simple lock.

But I was determined. It was important. I decided to break into the beach house. I could definitely climb over the short beach-house walls. I could then move from house to house. The man in the black car didn't see my face. If I just walked along the street as a civilian, he wouldn't know the difference. But I would have to be careful.

Maybe when I got there I could do the things I said I would to his wife.

The black car was parked in front when I got there. I parked four blocks away, on a corner, and looked into the distance. When I saw him there watching the street like I was watching him, I started having second thoughts. It was too risky. There was no fun in getting caught. I sat in the car and waited, trying to resolve my conflicted mind. Part of my mind was saying, 'Don't go, you'll get caught and this will be all over and you haven't done half of what you said you would do.' The other half was saying, 'Fuck him, he deserves it.' Lately the latter half was winning the argument.

The decision was made for me. Griffith himself walked out of the front gate and locked it. He gave the man in the black car a small wave. I had never seen Griffith in person. He was shorter in real life, like people always said about actors. He was wearing black jeans, black shoes and a black jacket over a navy blue button-down shirt, shiny like silk. From where I was sitting I could see circles under his eyes. No make-up in the real world. Maybe I was wearing on him.

He opened the garage with a key and went inside. The black BMW rolled out. His wife was in the passenger side. They drove in my direction. The man in the black car stayed where he was. I followed Griffith.

He drove on PCH towards Santa Monica. I watched people double-take him when they saw who was driving next to them. More than one person waved. I had a little trouble following him because the traffic was heavy, but I kept with him. My eyes were on the black glossy back of his car and his license plate: 'GR8ACTR.' I didn't realize at first that it was a vanity plate. Great Actor. What kind of sick, conceited fuck was I dealing with? He beat a yellow light. I sped through right as it turned red.

He took the Santa Monica freeway to Westwood where he drove deeper towards the Hollywood sign. His driving was slow and easy, as if he was afraid of losing control and jeopardizing his happy life.

At La Ciénega he got off and drove towards the mountains. I kept three cars back so he wouldn't recognize me. There were so many cars in LA he probably didn't know the difference.

He hit Sunset and turned left. The traffic was slow and more people were recognizing him. 'Hey Griffith,' a guy wearing a baseball hat shouted out of a pick-up. Griffith sped up.

Finally, at a quiet section of Sunset, full of posh shops and fine dining, he stopped and pulled into a parking lot. The valet took his car and shook his hand. Griffith and his wife started walking, both wearing sunglasses.

I was so focused on them that I didn't realize I was stopped in the middle of the street. A row of cars started honking. Griffith gave a quick look over but continued walking. I couldn't find a place to park. Fucking Los Angeles, there wasn't ever a place to park.

Then, a real stroke of luck. A car was pulling out of a space a block ahead. I sped there, keeping Griffith in my view so I could see where he was going, and I locked myself into the space. I didn't pay the meter. Griffith was walking into a restaurant as I got out of my car. The restaurant stretched half a block and was low to the ground. Smiling LA people sat at the tables outside.

Griffith didn't reappear. He must have gotten a table inside, away from the heat. I waited in my car forty-five minutes, an hour, while he ate. The sun was baking the car and inside it smelled like old-car plastic. My clothes were sticking to the seat. He dined while I sweat.

I didn't know what I was doing, sitting there, waiting for Griffith. I couldn't just go up to him and tell him all the things I wanted to say. Maybe I could. Or I could throw calves' blood on him like I wanted to do to his house. I had made the decision. I knew a butcher who sold calves' blood. Some people used it for cooking. I remembered being confused as hell when I saw 'Calves' Blood – $1.50 a cup' at the butcher shop and that stayed in my memory. I wanted to throw the calves' blood all over his clean porch or his front door, leaving a short note.

But I couldn't go up and do that to him, go into the restaurant and throw the calve's blood on his fine clothes. I can't say how much I wanted to, but I would have gotten easily caught. The waiters or other customers would quickly come to his highness's aid. It was safer and just as impacting if I went about it at a distance.

A car pulled up next to mine. The driver was shouting something at me. I rolled down the window.

'What?'

'Are you coming or going?'

'I'm staying here.'

'Then why don't you get out of the fucking car?' He drove off.

That happened more than once while I sat there. Such a happy city. LA was as bright as the sun, as dark as hell at night.

Soon Griffith and his wife came out of the restaurant. They walked towards the parking lot. I waited. The BMW pulled out of the lot and they turned left on Sunset, in my direction.

I followed them again. They ended up in Brentwood, twenty minutes from the Hollywood restaurant. They parked their car in an outdoor mall. I circled the lot until I could do the same.

They were just coming out of a pizza place as I found a spot. I didn't know why the hell they went there, they had just come from a restaurant. Everybody who saw them stopped, speechless, and gawked. Griffith and his wife walked on with contented faces, like nobody was watching them at all. But they knew. They had to. Griffith and Culver ignored everybody with an air of royalty importance. They were heading towards a flower shop when someone had the guts enough to ask for an autograph. As soon as that happened, everyone else felt relaxed enough to do the same. Soon there were nine people standing in front of them. I got out of the car to get a closer look.

Griffith smiled obligingly and started signing autographs with a silver pen that he probably had in his pocket, always at the ready to give his beloved name. A signature for Chrissakes. People's priorities were frightening. I stood against a tall lamp-post, ten feet away, and watched.

'What are you doing now, Mr Griffith?'

'I loved your last film.'

'I love all your movies.'

'You too, Robin.'

'Make that out to Samuel.'

More people were approaching. Griffith kept signing without a flinch or a wince, just an actorly smile.

I got back into my car and started it up. It had an old-car roar.

I started driving towards the crowd. Maybe I would drive up on the sidewalk and hit him. I didn't know what I was going to do. I could kill him right there, sever the relationship, end the suffering. But the crowd was in front of Griffith and Culver and I didn't feel right about hitting other people.

I rolled my window down. I hung my arm out the window, the sun hot against it. I was almost there.

I drove up alongside Griffith and his public. I yelled, all unrehearsed, but deeply part of my gut.

'You are nothing Griffith. You are a false idol and your day will come. I hope you like it in hell.'

He looked up, confused, sad even. So did the crowd. Some people were so confused that they looked all around them, as if the sound had come from the sky.

I drove quickly away. People were pointing at my car. Robin Culver's consoling eyes were on Griffith. Griffith's eyes stayed on my back fender. He wouldn't see a license plate. I had taken it off after I was chased by his attack bodyguard dog.

The balding tires of my car screeched for good effect. Just like up on screen. Sometimes life could be just as good as the movies.

Chapter Eighteen

FAVORITE SON

THERE WAS A note under the door when I got back to my apartment.

'Someone who says he's your father has been shouting from door to door looking for you. He's up in our apartment. Please come and get him. Joe and Daisy Palmer 208.'

I knocked on the door. Daisy, the housewife who I sometimes talked to, opened the door. She looked tired and apologetic. Her hair was not quite blond, not quite gray, almost a dull copper.

'Hello, Ray, he's right in here.'

I walked into the apartment. It was plain and sparse, a few pieces of furniture, a large TV, a couple of family pictures on the walls. I saw the back of my father's head sitting in a green chair. Joe Palmer sat in an easy chair facing me. He was thick and sweaty and gripping each arm of the chair with his heavy hands.

'So, Ray,' he laughed, 'is this your father?'

My father turned around. He looked like he'd gone through a Jekyll and Hyde transformation. His hair wasn't combed, his eyes bugged out and he grinned at me with those big teeth he had. So big they almost didn't look real. A thin cut was running down his cheek.

'Yeah, that's my dad,' I said.

'We weren't sure. He kept calling you Shark and he didn't know where you lived.'

'Shark is a childhood nickname,' I said. Shark was a name I got from the little league ball-field. I got the ball like a predator.

'Finally, he told us your name was Ray.'

'C'mon, Dad, let's go downstairs,' I said to the back of his head. I felt like I was talking to a man in a wheelchair.

My father got out of his seat and threw his hands down on the armrests. Dust flew into the air. Joe laughed nervously. Daisy stood next to him. I took my father by the back of the arm and brought him to front door. He didn't say good-bye to Joe and Daisy. His back remained to the apartment.

'Sorry about this,' I said to the husband and wife.

'It's not a problem,' Joe said.

Daisy looked at me sadly, said, 'Bye-bye,' in a pitying way and closed the door behind me.

I brought my father downstairs. I told him to sit on the couch and not touch anything while I went to the bathroom. I could hear him knocking around. Something hit the floor with a thump.

When I got back from the bathroom, my father was at my desk reading part of a letter I didn't send. My stapler lay at his feet.

'What's this?' he said.

'That's nothing.'

'What's this about you wanting to kill this guy? Is this a joke?'

'No, it's just something I'm writing.'

He put down the letter and looked at me. 'You're not into anything funny, are you?'

'No. I'm writing that because—' I stopped. 'It's part of a story I'm writing.'

'A story? You've never written any stories.'

'Well, I am now. I've become a writer. Take my word for it.' My voice was shaky. I tried to be calm but he made me nervous. He always made me nervous.

'Stories,' he said.

He stared at me strangely like he was trying to figure out what color eyes I had from far away.

'What's going on with you upstairs anyway?' I asked him.

'Nothing,' he said. He looked down. Good, I got his mind on other things.

'You know where I live.'

'I forgot.'

'Yeah? You've been here twenty times.'

'I've been forgetting a lot of things.'

'What, you're going senile?'

'No, it's not that, it's just that, shit, I don't know.' He clutched my letter absentmindedly in his hand.

'What is it?'

'Janice has got me all worked up.'

'You shouldn't let her do that to you.'

'She's tearing me up, Ray.'

'Give yourself a break.'

'Right.' He looked down at my brown carpet.

'How'd you get that cut on your face?' I said.

'What cut?' He felt his face all over with one hand.

'Right there, on your cheek.'

He felt again.

'The other one.'

He found the cut and began running his finger on it, up and down, as if he had no idea there was a four-inch-long gash, new and bright, running from his mouth to his sideburn like an extended smile.

'I don't know where I got it. Any number of places.'

He kept rubbing the cut. He stared straight ahead, his brain obviously working faster than his eyes.

'What do you want here?' I said. 'I mean, what's going on?'

'A number of things. For one, I think I might be going a little crazy. I don't know what it is, I've just been having a little trouble. I'll leave you alone if you want.' There was apologetic defeat in his voice. Not the deep, stern voice of the man who had intimidated me as a kid. 'I'm man enough to figure out these problems on my own,' he said.

'What problems?'

'Like I said, it doesn't matter.'

'Then why did you come over today?'

'I was in the neighborhood. I thought I'd stop by.' He laughed lightly. He was joking.

'Really,' I said. I felt like father over son.

'I don't know, Ray. I don't know why I came over.'

We were silent for about five minutes. I took the letter from his hands and put it on the TV. Then I sat on the couch and watched him tensely massage his palms, listening to the quiet, absolutely unsure of any solace I could give the old man. He hadn't quite taught me how to give or receive comfort.

'Well, I guess I'll be leaving,' he finally said.

'All right,' I said.

'We'll talk some other time. Real father–son.' He didn't sound convincing, his voice a brittle croak.

He got up. I didn't make a motion for him to stay. I didn't really want him there. I hadn't forgiven him yet for throwing that brick. I hadn't forgiven him for quite a lot.

He was at the door. I opened it for him. We were the same height but now he was bent over like a hunchback, shoulders at his neck as if in a perpetual shrug. His eyes were a full six inches below mine.

Before he left, he said, almost out the door, now looking at me dead-straight in the eyes, 'Be careful with those letters. They can get you into trouble.'

He then took a left on the street.

A few days later I got a strange phone call. Bud Friedman from college security called me again. 'We got him,' he said. 'We got the kid who was sending the letters to that girl. I just thought I'd call to let you know.'

'What?' I said. That's all I could say.

'Well, we put a statement about it in the weekly paper. The girl agreed to it. She wanted us to. The second week out, a kid confessed. Another student.'

'Oh yeah?' I almost said, 'Why?'

'I just thought I'd let you know.' He paused. 'I didn't

want you thinking that you were suspect. After the last time we talked.'

'No, no,' I said.

'This is one screwed-up kid, I've got to say. He was really anxious to confess.' Bud sounded proud. He had solved the case. 'The girl feels better now,' he said.

'Th—that's good,' I stammered.

I didn't know how to react. Part of me wanted to tell him I wrote the letters. Get credit where credit was due. But I didn't do that. I didn't say anything.

'How are you anyway?' he asked after my silence.

'Me? I'm fine.'

'You got a new job?'

'Yeah. I'm doing fine. I'm thinking of maybe becoming a cop.' I have no idea why I said that.

'Oh yeah?' he replied. 'That's good to hear.'

There was another silence. I could hear him writing. He said, 'Well, take care. I've got some phone calls to make over this. The Dean is going to call the kid's parents. I kind of feel sorry for him. He's got a lot of troubles. I'll see you,' he said happily.

We said good-byes.

I hung up and thought, 'How utterly goddamn confusing.' This was really too bad in a way because I was going to write Helen another letter. Nothing threatening. I was just going to tell her that I'd found somebody else. I didn't need her anymore. I had new prospects. But somebody beat me to it. I wasn't going to write the letter because I didn't want to get the kid in any more trouble than he already was.

An innocent kid confessed. What a crazy fuck.

I went back to the Bel-Air house to talk to the maid. I stood outside seven hours waiting for her to come out, from just before noon until sundown, watching rich silver cars go by and the sun change places over the mansion.

At dusk, she finally came out. She walked over rigid and

straight like a march. She wasn't wearing a coat and holding a purse like last time.

She came up to the gate but didn't open it.

'You have to leave,' she said.

'What?'

'You have been here too long, you have to leave.'

'I do?'

'Yes, you can't be here so long.' She had such a sweet Spanish accent.

'Why not?'

'We've been watching you. You have been here all day.' Her hands were placed sternly on her hips.

'But why do I have to leave?'

'Mr Griffith needs his privacy.'

'I thought Mr Griffith wasn't here.'

She looked at me as if I was a vicious stray dog.

'That doesn't matter. This is his home.' She kicked the ground. Maybe there were tears in her eyes.

'But I'm just standing here.'

'Please go,' she pleaded.

'We had such a nice talk the other day,' I smiled.

'Most people come for a short time and then leave. You have already seen the house. What do you want to see?'

What do I want to see? I want to see this house burn to the ground, with Griffith in it.

'Mr Griffith won't be here today, he's somewhere else.'

'At his beach house.'

'Yes. How—'

'What about our talk the other day?' I repeated.

'I don't know. Please leave.'

'Would you like to get some coffee? Maybe we could have some coffee inside.'

'I will have to call the police if you don't leave. They are prepared to deal with people like you.'

'People like me? What people like me?'

She stared at me hatefully, like a puzzle with one piece missing.

'Fine,' she said and started walking back towards the house.

'Come back here,' I yelled. 'We can be friends.'

She didn't turn around. She went back into the house through a side door. I saw that the black outer gate of the side door was shaped like a flower.

Everything was quiet for a few minutes while I stood there with my hands on the gate. I rang the doorbell and yelled into the intercom, 'There are no people like me. I am an original. I am the only one who really knows anything.'

I didn't know if they could hear me. There was silence again. Complete silence, as if the whole neighborhood was empty.

I heard a siren in the distance and wondered if it was coming my way. I wasn't about to wait and see. I got back into my car and drove off.

No fooling around now. I bought the calves' blood at the butcher shop, four cups of it in a large white plastic container. No questions asked by the butcher. The container was warm in my hands. I drove home with the container sitting next to me like a passenger. Once inside my apartment, I opened the lid. The blood was so red it was black. It smelled almost alive, like the flesh of a cow just killed. I put my nose so close to the container that some of the blood touched my lips. It was warm, a little thicker than water. Then I took a sip, a small one, then a larger sip. It tasted almost sweet, like thick water. I could feel it running down my body and mixing with my own blood. It felt right. Then I took a big sip, my head tilted back. I went into the bathroom and looked in the mirror. My lips were a deep red. The blood was stuck on my upper lip like a mustache. I thought about washing my face but I left it red. I stuck my hand in the container and pulled it out. It was covered with blood and dripping as if I had reached inside my body with my fist, touched my heart and taken my hand out. I wiped my hand all over my face until it was completely red. Like war paint. I stared at my eyes in the mirror. They seemed to be shaking. That was one strange sight. My goddamn eyes were shaking. And they were reflecting back two images of my blood-red, smiling face. My teeth looked paper-white next to the blood. I closed my eyes and breathed heavy. I was ready. I could have drunk all the blood right then. I could have bathed in it. But I wanted to save it for Griffith.

I was going to throw blood all over Griffith's front door, or maybe his back porch. Somewhere he lazed around in the comfortable, Malibu sun. Somewhere shocking and memorable. And nearby I would leave this note:

> *You can't escape me Griffith. I am inside. Like blood. I am inside your precious house. You are going to learn about the real world. Real people suffer, don't forget that. Make a public statement about how you are shallow and don't understand the struggles of real life, or quit the movies. If you don't, I will always haunt you. Maybe I will hurt you.*

But first I had to get inside.

I drove to the beach house again. The black car was there but I had other ideas. I parked the car far out of the way and walked towards the beach.

I walked along the wet sand, almost to the water. In the houses next to Griffith's no one seemed to be home. People didn't use these houses every day of the week. They stayed in their other mansions. This section of beach was nicer than where I lived in Venice. There was no sewer line that gave the swimmers cancer running into this beach. There were no beer bottles or empty wrappers sticking out of the sand. There were no homeless or screaming families. It was as serene as the sky. I felt the heat of the sand through the soles of my shoes. I was wearing long pants, only half cotton so they stuck to me. My light-blue button-down shirt was unwashed and stained. The sleeves were rolled up. My forearms were as dark with dirt as an auto mechanic's.

I saw Griffith's three-building mansion up ahead. The buildings were sunk back from the beach, unlike the other beach houses which were stuck right up on the beach. His had a deep front porch and yard. I caught a glimpse of a pool and a diving board and a small building which I guessed was a pool house. So like Griffith to have a pool next to the ocean.

I was one house away.

'Hey,' a voice shouted. I stopped where I was. A muscular, gray-haired man wearing shorts and a white T-shirt was pointing at me. He stood in front of the house next to Griffith's.

'This is a private beach.'

Dumbly, I found myself standing in the middle of the beach in plain view.

'I'll call the cops if you don't get off this beach.'

I looked down at myself. I looked bad. Fully clothed, in the middle of the beach, holding a large plastic container.

'I'm calling them right now.'

He went back into the house. For a second I thought about throwing the blood at him. But I ran the other way.

I went back to my car and waited. I didn't hear any sirens. I tried to control my heavy breathing, my heart beating every quarter second. I thought maybe I was getting high blood pressure. My breathing was unhealthy. It was the second time someone had threatened the cops on me in one day. That thought made my heavy breathing deepen and I considered leaving. But I still had work to do.

I walked towards the third house from Griffith's. The man in the black car couldn't see me because the third house was on the corner. The wall was about as tall as Griffith's front wall. In one motion I climbed over the wall, the calves' blood in one hand, vaulting with the other. I stood in a backyard. There was a pool with a brown stone edge in front of me. Behind that there was a brick porch. Large windows opened onto the porch. The lights were off in the house. Nobody seemed to be home.

I ran through the backyard to the other side of the house. The calves' blood splashed in the plastic jar. I climbed over the wall.

Then I ran through the next backyard as fast as I could and made it to the other wall. Some lights were on but I didn't think anybody saw me. There were bushes on the other side of the wall. I made my way over and into the bushes. I was pushed up against the wall, hot branches pressing into my face and body. I was trapped and sweating. Some of the bushes had thorns. I found an opening a few feet to my left and went through. As soon as I was out my body began to itch and sting.

It was the house of the guy who had yelled at me. I could see him walking through the living room, a dark silhouette with a drink in its hand. He lingered in the living room for a few seconds and then went to a back room I couldn't see, and where he probably couldn't see me. If I'd wanted to I could have gone in the house and taken his life. The sliding back door was wide open.

The house was low to the ground and I could feel the wind from the beach. It smelled of hot sand and salty water. In the backyard there was a pool shaped like a triangle. A triangular pool. I should have gone in there.

I ran across the yard.

I was hot and covered with dirt. Angry that I had to go through all this. I was at Griffith's wall. In front of me was a tall black gate similar to the one in front of his Bel-Air home. I knew immediately there was no way to get over it.

Chapter Nineteen

THEY

I WAS DEPRESSED again. My efforts with Griffith were going nowhere. My efforts with everything were going nowhere. My job, my friends, my parents. Marta, my best friend, was almost a distant memory. I didn't even have a chance.

There were days when nothing was happening with Griffith at all. I went by the Bel-Air house a few times but the Spanish maid didn't come out. I went to the beach house again to see if I could spot Griffith but I never did. The calves' blood sat in my refrigerator.

I was sitting in bed one night when I thought They would disapprove of what I was doing. They watched over while I did everything. When I brushed my teeth They scolded me if I put too much toothpaste on the brush. While I watched TV They told me if I had the volume too loud. 'Are you crazy?' They said. 'Act sensible.' When I drove my car They told me if I was driving too close to the car ahead. 'Other people don't drive that close. You don't want to look bad in the eyes of other people.' When I wrote my letters They told me what was right and what was wrong. I was constantly being monitored. Judged by a jury of my peers.

I'd always had inner conflict. As a kid I'd berate myself wickedly if I dropped the ball in a game or in high school if I didn't get the girl, which was often. I'd have an argument in my head as if talking to a separate voice. It was almost like having an imaginary friend except that the friend never left the back of my eyes. He wasn't a very good friend at all because he only showed himself when I was failing, never when I had done well. This wasn't a crazy kid at work, only a kid who was hard on himself.

But now the voice had grown. The voice had become something of a government. There was the president, who was the same voice I had as a kid, and now there were his offspring – cabinet members, secretary of state, department of defense, department of finance, judicial branch, house and senate.

Somehow, though I had become an adult and started shaving, the voice had stayed a child. Probably because I never wanted to grow up. The years before my tenth birthday were a smooth time. I didn't have many memories from that time – only short, blurry fragments – because before ten I had nothing to worry about. The only memories that seemed to stay with me were sour memories, teenage acne and loneliness, parents fighting, trying to kill myself at thirteen and being thrown in the UCLA psychiatric ward where I felt at home with the other young suicides and eating disorders. There were happy memories, sure, but I didn't brood about them so they were forgotten. Early childhood was an unblemished time. So now I had a chorus of children giving me direction. I was taking advice from a government of little voices. They berated me just like when I was younger.

That night in bed They told me that all my efforts were useless. Even with all that I'd done, nothing had really changed. 'Griffith,' They said, 'still lives in that house, still drives that car. He's still making the same movies. He's not changing. And the world still loves him.' That meant I was failing. 'You don't want to seem a failure,' They said. 'Where has that ever gotten you before? The way things are going, you are going to lose to Griffith and he is still going to be rich and famous. You will still be poor and miserable and crowds will still be chanting his name. He will still represent everything We hate. You will have taught the world nothing except that you are a failure. You don't want to stay a loser, do you Ray?'

I tried to tell Them to shut up and that I'd do something. They laughed at me with their munchkin laughter.

That night I slept dreamless, but I woke up as if out of a dream.

I still had to go to work. I haven't said much about the job at the parking lot because there was nothing worth mentioning. Sitting in the ticket booth at my job was uneventful. Nothing happened. Nobody talked to me. Sometimes people even avoided looking at me. They made it clear that they were snobbishly avoiding my eyes. I was left alone.

One day, I was sitting in the booth watching a talk show I'd already seen about men who sleep around behind their girlfriends' backs, called 'Are Men Pigs?', when I heard whispering coming from somewhere in the parking lot.

'There you are,' said a small, gruff voice. I thought it was coming from the TV. Or maybe Them.

'There,' the voice said again.

I looked up in the direction of the whisper. I saw a huddled man at the far wall of the lot, sitting between a Mercedes and an old Datsun. I walked over to him. He was old and heavily wrinkled but his hair wasn't gray. He was wearing brown pants, a brown shirt and had brown hair. He was a brown man. There was a bald spot about the size of a saucer on the back of his head. He turned his head, looked over at me and smiled. He was on both knees, hunched over something crookedly, like Igor.

'What are you doing here?' I asked.

'I have something,' he said.

'What?'

He didn't answer and turned away.

'You can't be here unless you have a car on the lot.'

I hated sounding like a teacher or a parent, or a boss. I didn't care if he was there or not. But I had to do something. The manager was going to be coming back after his lunch break. The manager was five years younger than me and, like everybody I'd ever worked with, cared more about the job than he should have. He always came to the job in a clean uniform, a stainless, sea blue. He would jump on me for there being a homeless man in the parking lot. I didn't want to lose another job. Looking for a new job would interfere with all my plans.

'Look,' the old man said to me. He held up an alarm clock. He was breathing heavily and had a wide smile.

'You see this clock?' he said.

'Yeah.'

'It's a bomb.'

'A bomb?'

'Yes.'

He was smiling happily. I didn't believe him. His fingernails were black as if every one of them were bruised. BO rose from him like heat. He also smelled a little of fish.

Up close, his bald spot revealed a scar, pink and two inches long. The hair couldn't grow back in that area. I looked down at him with regret. I wished he would just move away without me having to ask him.

'You really can't be here,' I said.

'I can set this off,' he said. Heavy breaths.

'Please leave.'

He stood up. He couldn't have been five foot three. He walked a few feet and then sat on the silver Mercedes, on the clean, metal hood. He put his feet on the bumper. He was content and smiling like a child on a swing. He held up the clock like it was a smooth jewel.

I stared at him. He was a sad sight.

Just then, a woman holding two white shopping bags with handles walked towards us. She stopped at the Mercedes.

She was speechless. A homeless man was sitting on her car.

'What,' was all she said.

'I'm sorry. I'm trying to get him off your car.'

'Well, please do,' she said. She didn't even look at me. She didn't move.

'All right. Please get off the car,' I told him. I took the guy gently by the elbow. He smelled so strong I had to breathe through my mouth. He pulled his elbow away. I didn't want to be too forceful. I looked at him and nodded towards the woman. He looked back at me with a smile and with crazy eyes that said, 'It will take a bullet to get me off this car.' A bullet was probably what he wanted.

'Please get him off my car,' the woman said. She was getting testy. She covered her nose with her hand. She had purple-painted nails.

I grabbed the man by both arms. He shook away again and rolled to the other side of the hood.

'What are you, incompetent?' she yelled acidly.

I stopped and looked at the woman. She stared at me and the homeless old man with a sour look, her lips pinched together. She looked at her bags, then at her watch. 'Get *him* off my car. I have to go.'

I looked at her and then at the old man.

'I just had my car washed,' she said.

That's when I walked away.

'Where are you going?'

'Lady, fuck you.' I made a hard step towards her like I was going to hit her. She put up her arms and shrieked. I turned and walked back to the booth.

'I'll call your superiors,' she screamed.

'Fine.'

As soon as I walked away, the homeless man got off the hood. When I got back to the booth I saw that he was walking away from the car and scratching his balls with his hands deep inside his pants.

The woman got back into her car. She didn't say anything to me when she paid her six dollars and she drove out of the parking lot scowling.

Later I saw the man asleep in a doorway a block away. He wasn't holding the clock. The clock lay next to him. It was

smashed with the glass broken and arms bent. He was cradling
something else, a dark red bag.

That scene made me depressed as hell.

I needed to get going again. 'Need' was too light a word. I
wouldn't feel alive if I didn't do something else. I needed to get
going like a person *needed* to eat and breathe.

Seething, rhymes with breathing.

I looked for the papers for the apartment manager's job. I found
them in my desk, under some magazine articles about Griffith.
Scribbled at the top of the front page in black ink was David's
phone number. As much as I hated his Hollywood kind, I needed
him to get close to Griffith.

I dialed the number. He answered gruff, as if out of sleep.

'Did I wake you?' I said.

'No. Who is this?'

'Ray . . . Ray Tompkins, from the apartment.'

'Oh. Then you did wake me.' He laughed. 'What is it?
Something wrong with the apartment?'

'No. Something else.'

'What?'

I took in a breath. 'Is there any way for me to get a job on
a movie?'

'On my movie?'

'No, on . . . a Tim Griffith movie.'

'Why a Tim Griffith movie?'

'Because his are always the most successful, I figured that was
a good place to start.'

'I see.'

'I love that Tim Griffith.'

'Uh-huh.'

'So what do you think?'

'Well, I don't think you can just get a job like that,' he said.

'Why not?'

'You have to be in the union.'

'Oh.'

'Sorry.'

'Are you sure?' I asked.

'Yeah.'

'Dammit. Goddammit.' I swore just to make him agitated.

'Uh . . . I mean, I could check. But I doubt it.'

'Thanks. I'm getting sick.'

'Sick?'

'Of the job I've got now.'

'Oh.'

'I'd be real fucked if I couldn't get that job.'

'Well,' he stated. 'How's the managerial job?'

'It's fine.'

'Someone told me you weren't there a lot.'

'Who?'

'Someone upstairs. They said they tried to reach you about some electrical problems, but you weren't there.'

'I have a job,' I said.

'She came four different times.'

'I work a lot.'

'Try and be there. I've actually been meaning to call you about it.' There was thin complaint in his voice.

'Fine. Try and find out about that job on the movie set,' I said.

'OK. I will.'

'Make sure it's a Tim Griffith movie.'

'All right. But don't hold your breath.' He laughed. We hung up.

I sat on my living room couch, TV off, staring at the wall and feeling bad. I was slowly running out of options. I had done everything I could with letters. I tried my hardest to get into his houses. But he was still safe and secure like he shouldn't have been, preaching his rich and pretty gospel. Mine and Griffith's relationship was like a failing marriage, without growth. But like

Christ was married to the cross, something positive could result, resurrection. I wasn't a religious person, but I believed in what was right. The world could become a better place. Everybody would learn that I was a preacher of good faith and that Griffith was Judas. I was so eager and so upset because it was such an important prophecy to fulfill. But nothing was happening. I didn't know what to do.

Then, at a crucial moment when I was grabbing my hair until it hurt, I remembered the *Variety* article.

I went to the desk drawer where I pulled out the managerial papers. Underneath them were the articles I'd xeroxed about Griffith. I took the articles over to the couch. The *Variety* article was on top.

'Tim Griffith's new movie, *Heart of Bone*, will be filmed in and around Los Angeles. The first location will be the Italian restaurant Orologio. In order to use the restaurant for filming, they had to remove all the tables and chairs and replace them with tables and chairs of the forties' style. The film is a period piece set in post-war Los Angeles of the 1940s. Shooting starts Wednesday.'

It was Wednesday.

I looked up Orologio in the white pages. It was on a street I'd never heard of. I looked it up on the map. It was in Westwood, where all the movie theaters were.

I drove there, parked, and found myself in a crowd.

About a hundred people were standing around watching, but there was nothing to see. There was a black sheet hanging over the restaurant window. All the filming was being done inside. There were a few tall, stray lights standing just outside the restaurant. All anyone could see were the grunt workers carrying equipment to and from the trucks. Thick black, snake-like chords ran on the ground into the restaurant.

There were five trucks for equipment and three trailers for the actors. The equipment trucks were on the right of the restaurant and the trailers were on the left. There were plenty of cops. One stood in front of the restaurant looking out at the crowd.

I walked as close as I could to the trailers. On one door it said Haldeman, the other Johnson and then on the one furthest from me it said Tim Griffith with a gold star underneath, just like I had imagined.

I waited awhile. I watched the grunt workers with beefy arms, all wearing shorts and short-sleeve shirts. They looked more determined and self-important than if they had been lifting warehouse boxes. They knew they were being watched. The crowd was looking at them because there weren't any stars to watch.

Nothing happened for quite some time.

Then the actress named Debra Haldeman got out of her trailer. The crowd stirred, a collective sigh. She walked, head down, towards the restaurant. She seemed freak-like, nervous and afraid. A giant sun-like spotlight called attention to her every move. Everyone else at the set was faceless, but her face was known by all these hundreds of prying eyes.

I waited for Griffith. He wasn't anywhere to be seen.

All the trailers were parked against the curb. I could reach them if I edged my way forward through the crowd. A cop stood at the far end of Haldeman's trailer. The trailers went Haldeman, Johnson, Griffith. I was already in front of Johnson's. The other cop who was standing in front of the restaurant was looking the other way, fifteen feet from Griffith's trailer.

I walked swiftly toward Griffith's truck and laid down my letter on the top step as if I were laying down a bouquet of flowers. The letter only had five words:

I'm here.
I'm watching you.

I pushed the letter close to the door.

I could have been anybody. I was showered and dressed in clean clothes. I could have been a messenger. I could have been on the crew. I could have been a fan who just wanted to deliver a nice message. Nobody noticed me.

I made my way back into the crowd. I waited and waited, staring at Griffith's trailer.

A group of kids walked by looking serious, proud of being at a movie set. They were frowning and walking tall as if they had been let in on a tough secret.

Most of the crowd were dressed for the beach. All white shirts with beachwear logos and shorts. The couple next to me were bronze and smiling, standing on their toes to see what was happening. She only wore a bikini top and short shorts. He was muscular and held her shoulders. His hands were covered with golden hair. There must have been twenty other couples who looked the same. Griffith's fans. Watching their vacant, hopeful faces, I knew *some*body had to be taught a lesson.

'I don't think he's going to come out,' the guy said.

'Maybe he's already in there,' she said back.

'We'll see him,' I assured them. They scowled and looked me up and down like I had ruined their privacy.

The couple eventually got tired and left. I waited in the same spot for hours. Some new faces came but they got lazy and left as well. The crowd got thinner. The crowd was now only about thirty.

I had to stay around. I wanted to see Griffith's expression when he saw the letter, just like I had watched Helen open her letter from behind the glass door. I wanted to see his look of fright.

The day was still hot but it was nearing dusk. Most people got bored and went away. Then Griffith finally came out. He walked from the restaurant in the direction of the trailer. People cheered. They cheered with a strange, high-pitched kind of shriek, almost like scared animals. It sounded like 'eeeee.'

But then I didn't hear their shrieking anymore. The only sound that filled my brain was the thick vacuum of silence as I watched Griffith.

Griffith looked poor. He looked overworked and tired. He was wearing thick, beige make-up. His forehead was shiny from sweat. He was wearing an old brown suit from the forties which made him look twice his age. He looked dead and gray. I felt good.

'Griffith,' I started screaming. Low, but loud and gruff. 'All right, Griffith.' It was loud enough that he looked over in my direction. He waved with a slight smile. The crowd's cheers got louder.

I clapped my hands until my palms stung.

'All right, Griffith. Way to go, Griffith. Wooeee.' I was yelling. The people next to me looked over. Some even moved away.

He opened the door to his trailer. Before he went inside, his hand on the doorknob, he looked down. He saw the letter. He bent down to pick it up. He must have been very tired because he didn't think twice about it and walked into his trailer.

Soon, a pretty woman wearing a beige skirt and a white blouse walked very quickly to Griffith's trailer, holding her skirt to her legs. She knocked twice and went inside. She left after five minutes and then walked over to a cop standing in front of Haldeman's trailer. The cop left where he was standing and then ran somewhere I couldn't see. Two different cops, not the one who was standing in front of the restaurant and not the one by Haldeman's trailer, walked up to Griffith's trailer and stood in front of it, motionless.

I was done. I felt better. The security was tight, but Griffith was afraid.

The cops stood, arms crossed, like guards in front of a politician's hospital bed.

Chapter Twenty

NEVER LET A DOG PISS ON A MOTORCYCLE

ON THE WAY home something happened. I was walking to my car from the movie set through the busy Westwood streets when I saw a man walking his dog. He was thin with crew-cut hair, smooth-skinned and shiny. The dog was one of those show dogs with an unpronounceable name, fluffy brown and always smiling. The dog stopped and sniffed. The owner didn't look down because the dog stopped every ten feet. Using it like a hydrant, the dog took a piss on a motorcycle. It was one of those fluorescent Japanese models that looked like a racing bike. The dog mainly pissed all over the tire, making the tire a darker black. Yellow piss dripped off the spokes. The owner didn't notice it but a man was quickly walking their way. He was wearing wide, dark sunglasses, tight jeans and a T-shirt with high sleeves which showed off thick, strong arms. He seemed to be gritting his teeth and flexing those muscles.

The owner was just on a walk with his dog, letting his dog relieve himself. When the guy got to them, the dog was just finishing. The guy picked up the dog by the collar and held it in front of him. The dog's head started shaking, its tongue caught between its teeth. It looked like it was going to choke. The dog's owner slowly put out his arm, as if to softly stroke his dog, give it some comfort. The motorcycle driver then threw the dog at its owner. The owner put up his hands to protect himself and the dog fell to the ground on its side. The driver walked away. The dog lay there a second and its owner bent down, sobbing lightly and shaking like he'd just been robbed. The dog got up on all four legs and they very slowly walked away, as if afraid to move.

On my way home I stopped at a traffic light in Venice. I looked to my right. There was a gun store. I stared at it. But then I drove on.

A few days later I went to the library to check that day's *Variety*. If I was lucky, I'd find something on Griffith. Most days I wasn't lucky. That day I was. On page two there was an article with the headline 'Griffith Pic Set for Early Release.'

'Tim Griffith's new film, *The Lesser of Two Evils*, is set to be released in July instead of September because of early positive response from test groups. Because July is a stronger month for movies than September, MGM said today that they were going to release the movie early even if it goes against other big summer movies. The film premières July 8 in New York and July 10 in Los Angeles.'

I was proud of my last encounter with Griffith at the movie set. I felt I was wearing on him. But They still weren't happy. They said I wasn't doing enough. Griffith may have been afraid but he was still working on that movie set. And everyone cheering for him had no idea that he wasn't what he appeared to be. That he was a false idol. They told me that I had to do more. They were displeased. They were desperate. Something rash had to be done.

I went outside and got the phone number of the payphone outside my door. Then I went into my apartment, drew the curtain and sat down at the table by the window. I took the phone in my hands. I dialed the payphone number and peeked through the curtains like my mother had peeked on my dad. The phone started ringing outside. I could hear the ringing from my apartment. The sidewalk in front of my apartment was usually busy. Someone would pick up. A man carrying a small suitcase walked by the phone. He stared at it but walked on. A jogger wearing a Walkman ran by. Then a woman, slightly overweight, stepped up to the phone and picked up.

'Hello?' she said.

'I know all about you. You are going to lose.'

'W—what?'

'I've been watching you.'

She hung up. She looked around her, left to right, then she walked quickly away.

I waited five minutes until she was far away and I dialed again. A man and a woman walked by. They looked at each other with puzzled expressions but they kept on walking. Then a man walked up. He was wearing pressed black pants and a white shirt rolled past his elbows. He looked like a businessman at ease. He picked up the phone.

'I know your kind. Your kind is going to die.'

He hung up quickly and took off, almost a slow jog, scratching his head hard with two fingers.

I dialed again. The man with the suitcase came by again and this time he picked up.

'Hello?'

'You are lost. You are going to lose.'

'Who is this?'

'Give up. I am watching.'

He hung up and walked away. He almost forgot his suitcase.

I was tired. That shut Them up long enough so I could get some sleep. I went into my room and lay down.

I went back to the movie set. They were still filming inside the restaurant. But this time they were filming in the back area which wasn't completely enclosed. I could catch glimpses of Johnson, Haldeman and, most importantly, Griffith walking by the opening. A guy who I figured was the director pointed and gave orders from a chair.

For some reason, Griffith looked happy today. The pale deadness of the other day was gone. He was smiling and energetic, as if he'd come into some good news. His pretty face was as bright as ever.

That smile felt like splinters all over my body. In every tooth I saw Helen sleeping with her young boyfriend, Marta going down on Bill, Sherry with Don and a hundred other porn-star men. I saw jobs gone stale and parents who hated each other. People who hated themselves. Every smiling tooth told a story.

Something had to be done.

The time was twelve o'clock. The set had to stop for lunch soon. Maybe Griffith would venture out into the public. The public would be waiting.

I paced across the street, back and forth, staring at the gap in the black curtain.

Then, and I almost couldn't believe it, I saw him leave out the back way with an older woman. I couldn't tell at first but then I realized it was his mother. I had seen a picture of her in one of the articles. She was an attractive older woman with reddish hair who probably had been beautiful when she was younger. Now she was a handsome woman. She had a famous air about her because I'd seen her glossed up in a magazine, a look of self-fulfillment and pride. Griffith had the same look of pride as his mother. I guessed he'd inherited it. They walked in the opposite direction from me.

I had an idea. A good idea. My car was parked in the parking lot right behind me. I ran to get it and drove off. I gave the booth operator a five dollar bill and didn't wait for my change.

I got into the street and began driving slowly. I found Griffith and his mother walking on the sidewalk, right in broad daylight. No one else was around. I followed behind them slowly, like a prowling cat about to pounce on a bird, or a rat.

They crossed the street right in front of me on the crosswalk. I could have pounced on him right then. But there was something I had to do first. I had to meet him.

I drove up to the intersection. They were in the middle of

the crosswalk. I honked. Not politely, a 'Get the fuck out of my way' honk.

He stopped and looked at me.

'Hello, Mr Griffith,' I said.

He smiled and said, 'Hello,' as if I was anybody, just another fan.

'No,' I said. 'I mean, hello, Mr Griffith.'

I thought he might have understood who I was because he made a quick step as if he was going to run away. Then he looked at his mother. She probably couldn't do any running.

'Hi, Mrs Griffith,' I said politely.

'Hello,' she said in a friendly way.

I was only five feet away from him. Above the heat of the street I could smell him. All make-up and nervous sweat.

'Who are you?' he asked.

'Who am I? You know who I am.'

'I know . . .' He double-took me as if he had tried to block out all my letters and then suddenly remembered.

'I've been speaking with you.'

'Yes,' he said simply. He didn't move. He looked left to right as if to call someone. But there was no one to call. And he probably didn't want to bring any more attention to himself than he already did by having his face.

'You have a fine son,' I told his mother.

She looked at Griffith. Her son looked afraid. She asked him, 'Who is this?'

'It's him,' he said.

His mother mouthed the word 'Him.'

The word resonated like a happy song.

'You bet,' I said. 'It's me.' I tapped the side of my car with my fingers, than rearranged the side mirror. For a second I saw myself, brightly smiling. Then I moved the mirror away. 'And I am going to have to put you in the hospital.'

I sped ahead and nearly hit him as I did. Griffith and his

mother didn't waste any time walking back toward the set. I watched Griffith look at me over his shoulder. As I drove away, I wondered how I was going to act on those last words I'd said.

I thought it went well.

Phone call.

'Hello?'

'Ray?'

'Yes.'

'This is Sherry.'

'Sherry?'

'Cherry Blossom.'

'Oh.'

'How are you?'

'I'm fine.'

'I've got some bad news.'

Other than talking to you on the phone? 'What?'

'Do you remember Joyce?'

'Yes.'

'You do?'

'I remembered you, right?'

'Yeah. Well,' she paused and sniffed. 'Joyce died.'

'She did? What happened?'

'She . . . was beat up.'

'By who?'

'A man.'

'Was she mugged?'

'No, she, I'd rather not say.'

'What?' I yelled. The information slowly sank in and, for some reason I couldn't explain, this was a heavy, heavy shock. It was almost like hearing Marta had died. I didn't know why. Maybe because I didn't know too many women.

'A man beat her up,' Cherry said.

'Was he from the set?'

She paused. 'No. Not really. He's an old boyfriend. They had got back together.'

'Do you know who it is?'

'That doesn't matter. I'm just calling to tell you the news and about the funeral.'

I had to smile slightly at how strange and bad this news was.

'I want to know what happened,' I said.

'I can't tell you. Please.'

'I think I should know. I have a right to know.'

'He didn't mean to kill her. He was just pushing her around and he got rough and, you know.'

'I know?'

'Yeah.'

'Do you know who it is?' I repeated.

Reluctantly, 'Yes, I do.'

'We should do something about this.'

'There's nothing we can do.'

'Why not?'

'He's got many friends and . . . there's nothing we can do.' Defeated.

'Fuck him.'

'Look, I just called to tell you when the funeral is. She really liked you, Ray. I think she wanted you to know that.'

'She liked me?'

'She told me.'

'We saw each other twice.'

'Still, she liked you. She didn't see that many people.'

'Oh.'

'The funeral's going to be small. She doesn't have any family so it's just going to be some of her friends.'

'I can't go.'

'You can't?'

'No.'

'But I haven't told you what day it is yet.' She sounded like she was going to cry.

'It doesn't matter. I have things to do.'

'Are you sure?'

'Yes.'

'OK. I'm sorry.'

Sherry sounded beaten and worn. She had a tired crack in her voice. An old young girl. I then got a picture of her sitting on the bed, on the damp white sheets, right before she got up to take a shower. I couldn't shed the party memory I had of her. A strange, wavy flashback.

'Hey, Sherry?' I asked.

'Yeah?'

'How's Ron?'

'R – Ron? How do you know Ron?'

'You know, I met him at the party.'

'You did? Then you know all about him.'

'I do? What do you mean?'

'Well, that night at the party I heard Ron tried to push Joyce around.'

'He did? Ron Gold pushed Joyce?'

'Ron Gold?' she said. 'Who's – oh, you mean *Don* Gold. Ron is somebody else.' She sounded relieved.

I was confused but then a face suddenly came into my head. Towards the end of the party, after Sherry and Don Gold fucked, some fat guy named Ron started pushing Joyce around. He had thick arms and a surly face and he made Joyce nervous.

'Shit,' I said. 'Is this guy Ron the guy who killed Joyce?'

'I don't know. I'm not gonna say any more,' she said.

'Is he?' I was frantic. I was beginning to hear Their cheer-leader chants.

She gave a reluctant and nervous, 'Yes. It's him. But,' she was quick to add, 'he's got a lot of friends.'

'Friends.'

'Yeah. So he can get away with it.'

'Fuck his friends.'

'No,' she said.

'Is he in the business?'

'No. Not really. I mean, he's not in the business, but he's friends with people in the business. I don't know why she got back together with him. He's not a very good man.'

'Well, there aren't very many good men.'

She didn't answer that.

'Where does he live?' I said.

'I can't say.'

'Where,' I demanded. I was getting little chipmunk cheers of 'Yay!'

'Really, Ray, this isn't something you want to get involved in.'

I was already involved more than she knew. Up to my waist, sinking deep like in quicksand mud.

'Who would care if some stranger came and fucked with him?' I said. I needed to do this. I didn't even need Them telling me I should. My fists were aching for it like my fingers once did for the pen.

'They'd come after you,' she said.

'I don't care. He deserves it.'

She was quiet for a long time. 'OK,' she finally said. 'I'll give you the address. He lives in Mar Vista. 1600 Bridge Street.'

'1600 Bridge Street, you say?'

'Yeah,' she said regretfully, as if she'd made a bad decision.

'In Mountainview.'

'Mountainview? No, in Mar Vista.' She stopped and said, almost sweetly, 'That's all I'm gonna say.' But then she added, 'Joyce was addicted to uppers, you know.'

'No, I didn't.'

'She was.'

No wonder she was so fake happy all the time.

'I heard he filled her up with drugs and then beat her up. She was old, you know, frail. She—'

'Yeah,' I cut in. I wanted her to stop talking. 'Thanks for telling me all this.'

'Sure. I don't know why I did.'

Probably because in another ten years you're going to be where Joyce is now.

I asked bitingly then, 'How is Don Gold?'

'Don? Oh, I don't really know what he's doing now. I haven't seen him for a while.'

'OK. I'll see you.'

'Uh—'

'So long.' I hung up.

I imagined Tim Griffith pounding Joyce with his fists, slitting her wrists, hanging her from a rope, anything that degraded a person.

I changed my shirt, got my wallet, my keys and some gas pills for the gas pains I'd started having. It was four o'clock but I rubbed the sleep out of my eye. And then I went to the gun store.

Chapter Twenty-one

HOLD ME IN YOUR CHARTER ARMS

I DIDN'T GO to the gun store I passed on that drive home. There was one off Olympic in an old, brick building that looked like it would sell to anybody. I didn't have a record, but I didn't want to be hassled either.

I walked into the gun shop. Inside, there were racks of camouflage clothes, boots, camping gear, a wall of rifles and a glass case full of revolvers. The place was nicer than I had imagined, like a clean sporting goods store. The man at the counter was neatly dressed and fragile-looking, balding with soft eyes. I put both my hands on the counter like I was confronting him.

'I want to buy a gun,' I said.

'What kind?'

'A .38 caliber pistol.'

'All right,' he said. 'That's a fine choice.'

He took out five different models and laid them out on the case. They looked like heavy toys. I picked each one up to see how they felt. I chose one that was jet black and felt good in my hand. It wasn't too heavy but it wasn't too small. It fit my hand as if it was meant for my fingers.

'What are you going to use it for?' he asked.

'I—' I stumbled my words. I was a little nervous. The rifles on the wall stared down at me like the heads of killed animals.

'I have to ask that, you see.'

'Protection. I just need it for protection.'

'That's what I thought.'

That wasn't so far from the truth. I wrote my name, address, birthdate and place of birth on a form. 'I'll be back soon,' he said. 'I have to go check on this.' He went into the back of the store.

It took some time. I didn't browse. I just waited. 'You're fine,' he said when he came back. 'That gun is two hundred and fifty dollars.'

It was all the money I had in the world. The money I'd saved from the parking lot and the free rent. I could have bought a cheaper gun but none of the others felt so right in my hand, not even the ones that were more expensive.

'Now, there's a fifteen-day waiting period to buy that gun.'

'Fifteen?'

'In California there's a fifteen-day waiting period.'

'But I don't have a record.'

'It doesn't matter. You have to wait.'

'Why?' I asked, an angry plead.

'I guess they think it will stop somebody from doing something,' he said. 'Gives them time to think it over.'

'But I need a gun for this weekend.'

'Are you going hunting?'

'Yeah.'

'I thought you said it was for protection.'

'It's for both.'

'Oh.' He looked at me skeptically.

'Can't you just sell me the gun?'

'No. I can't do that.'

'Look at me. I'm safe.' I looked down at myself. I could have been cleaner.

'I don't run that kind of business. Either you wait the fifteen days or you don't buy it.'

I tried to stare him down.

'Look, I don't much like the law either. It costs me business,' he said, a little stern, a little sad. He wasn't going to budge.

I turned and walked out of the store, slapping a mannequin dressed in scuba gear as I left. It rocked until it almost tipped over. The owner yelled, 'Hey,' as I got out on the street.

I knew about a few pawn shops. I didn't know why I hadn't thought of that first. I went back to Venice and traveled the pawn shops. The first one had nothing, just old typewriters and musical equipment. The second one had four guns displayed in a glass case just like the gun shop.

'Do you have a .38?' I asked.

The man behind the counter stared at me. He was old but he wasn't frail. He had an angry face, round and unshaven. He was dressed in a tight light-blue shirt and plaid pants with beer flesh pouring over his belt. There was a hole in his back pocket which I saw when he turned around. The whole shop smelled like cigar smoke. The old man scowled at me for no reason at all.

'Yeah, there's a .38 in there.' Almost as if to say, 'What of it?'

'Can I see it?'

He looked at me angrily again and then unlocked the case with a key off his belt.

He handed the gun to me sideways. I held the gun by the handle and pointed it at the floor.

'That's a Charter Arms pistol. It fires nice. I wouldn't sell a pistol that didn't fire nice.'

'How much is it?'

'That gun is,' he looked at me, 'two hundred dollars.'

'How about one-fifty?'

'No. Two hundred.'

'All I have is one-fifty.'

'No you don't. You're a bad liar.'

He was the one who was lying. I was a fine liar.

'I'm telling the truth. I walked in here with one hundred and fifty dollars. Maybe I'll be able to cover tax.'

He paused and eyed me like I was a gun. 'All right,' he said.

I handed him the money. I felt the gun in my hands now that

I owned it. It wasn't quite as good as the .38 at the gun shop but it fit my hand fine.

'Do you have any bullets?'

'Bullets?'

He stared at me darkly again. 'Yeah, I've got bullets to fit that. How many do you want?'

He pulled a box from the shelf behind him full of records, lunchboxes, TVs and other junk.

'I just need six. Just enough to fill the chamber.'

He pulled the box of .38 shells back from me.

'Why do you need only six?'

I looked up at him. He looked more skeptical than I'd seen him, maybe even a little afraid.

'May as well give me the whole box.'

'All right. We only sell them by the twenty.'

He sold me the bullets.

I gave him the money, five dollars my change and the old man said, 'Have a nice day.' I walked out carrying the gun and the box of bullets in a brown paper bag. That gun which felt heavy in my hand was going to change things.

I had only held a gun two times before in my life. I had experiences with guns like any young kid. When I was ten years old we had a gun in the house for protection. I remembered the day my father brought it home. My mom was upset like there was a death in the family. He told her that we had to have it. The bad neighborhood was creeping our way. A friend of my father's, named Mal, was mugged near our block. I didn't like Mal. He always hit me hard on the shoulder when he saw me. He was a big man and I was a little kid. I remembered being glad when I heard he got mugged. He was mugged coming home from someplace my parents would never tell me. I asked but they never would say. I figured out later that he was coming from the house of a woman who wasn't his wife. My parents said it didn't matter what Mal was doing. The mugger took his wallet.

The night my dad came home with the gun, he laid it down on

the dining room table. 'Ray, come here,' he said. 'I'll let you see this now because I'm here with you.' I looked at the gun sitting on the newly polished table which smelled of lemon. The gun was bigger than both my hands. It had a short black barrel and a fake wooden handle. I reached for the handle and touched it but my mom screamed, 'Get him away from that,' crying. My dad took it into the other room. I remembered thinking that the gun was cold. That was all I thought about it. It was cold. I never saw the gun after that night. I looked for it, even at the top of my parent's closet, but I never found it.

The second time I saw a gun was when I was sixteen. A friend of mine, Dan, found that same kind of gun in the top of his parent's closet. One summer day, we took it to a field. It was hard to find a field in Los Angeles so we drove as far north as possible. Los Angeles seemed to go on forever. We finally found a decent field where nobody would see us an hour and a half out of the city.

We shot at cans and rocks. I was pretty good at it. So was Dan. He aimed at the sky and hit a low-flying bird. It fell in a spiral towards the ground fifty feet away from us. We found it breathing heavily on the ground. Dan had only hit one of its wings. It lay there panting, its head in the dirt, breathing in dust. 'Kill it,' I said. He wouldn't do it. He looked the bird over, staring at it from every angle. I felt sorry for it. It lay there suffering. I took the gun from his hand and shot it. The bullet shot straight through so there wasn't a mess. It was the only thing I'd ever killed. I felt remorseful. But then I began to feel good in a way that I could kill something so easy and not get arrested.

Dan got yelled at like hell when we got back to his house. His parents were yelling so hard that they didn't even see me leave. I didn't see Dan for a couple of months after that, until school started. He was a different person. He had cut his hair and found a girlfriend. He started hanging out with her friends, students in the chamber orchestra, people out of my reach. We weren't very good friends after that.

I thought about that bird on the ride home from the pawn shop.

The bird didn't deserve to die. It wasn't doing anything but flying. Griffith was different. He was hurting people. By ignoring real people and living his grand, gleaming life, he was as violent as anyone. Ron was different as well. He was a killer himself. He wasn't nearly as important as Griffith but I had to do something to him. For Joyce, for anyone who lived their life with a frown. Anyone confused and alarmed. But mainly for myself.

When I got home I ran inside, paper bag in hand. Immediately I loaded six rounds in the chamber. I pointed the loaded gun at my desk. It felt right. Heavy as I'd remembered it.

Then I drove my way up to Mar Vista. It bordered Venice, a residential neighborhood of small houses, low to the ground, with backyards separated by cinder-block walls. The neighborhood was close to my apartment but with all the traffic the drive took me thirty-five minutes.

This was a good first step. I wasn't hearing any complaints from Them at all.

The guy's house looked something like Marta's, small and chipped. The lawn was faded green with an orange tree in the center. Tall, thin palm trees hung over the house in back.

I walked right up to the front door. I wasn't going to be as careful about this house as I had been with Griffith's. I didn't give a shit about Ron. He was nothing. So little that he shouldn't have been able to go on living.

There were hedges lining the path to the front door. I turned the knob. The door was open. I wondered if it would have been this easy at Griffith's house all along. I opened the door slowly. It opened into a small, carpeted living room. The house seemed to be empty. An indoor window looked into a kitchen to the left. There was only a black vinyl couch, a long coffee table and a weight set in the living room. No lamps, no plants, no bookshelves. Beyond the living room there was the porch which had a view of a short yard, the base of palm trees and the back of another house. The gun was in my right pants' pocket. It made me walk heavy on my right leg. I wanted to get this over quick. It was so obvious what I had to do, it was almost boring. Like busywork, lifting a box or walking around a campus. This was my new job.

Ron walked in the room then, whistling and wearing only a robe. I faintly recognized him from the party. He was hairy and looked serious in a criminal way. I couldn't understand what Joyce saw in him.

He saw me almost immediately. And he looked immediately angry. I was about to say, fake-friendly, 'Hello, Ron, How are you?' but he said, 'Who the fuck,' and he tore at me. I grabbed for the gun but I missed my pocket. And before I knew it I was on the ground and I was being hit. Mainly they were hits to the body. Very, very hard. He was professional. I wasn't much of a fighter. I never was. I felt pathetic, lying there like that, being hit with hard punches, feeling a pain like being rained on by bricks. I could feel myself immediately beginning to bruise.

But then I fixed myself. I pushed all his fat off of me. Like a person lifting a car when someone is trapped under it. What they called an emergency circumstance. He fell back. I got up quickly and reached for the gun. As soon as I reached down for the gun I stopped. It felt cold. Something wasn't right. It didn't feel right using that gun on somebody other than Griffith. That gun had only one purpose. I wanted to keep it virgin for the real villain.

So I hit him. Like I said, I wasn't much of a fighter, but right then I was. I hit him wherever I could, without aim. Tears came to my eyes.

'Goddammit,' he said.

The pain of him hitting me was washed away by the adrenaline. He fell down and I stood over him. I kicked him as if hitting a ball and trying to kick it ten miles. He made a dull groan. Blood was soaking through his white robe. He tried to get up. He got up halfway and fell back on the balls of his feet onto the empty coffee table. The table broke into equal halves.

When that happened, a tired female voice called from the bedroom in back, 'What the hell was that?' I started to leave.

But then I gave Ron one more look. He looked just fine. Sitting like a child, cross-legged, holding his head in his hands. He was so beaten, overtaken with bruises and pain, that he didn't even look up at me. He almost looked drunk.

I ran out of the house and to my car.

My head was spinning as I drove back down Venice Boulevard. I had finally done something for real. No more of just my pen spitting flame.

I was glad I hadn't used the gun.

When I got back home I wanted to call Marta. I was feeling better than I had been in a long time. I was finally focused.

The première was in five days.

I knew now that I had to kill Griffith. Letters weren't enough. While people like Joyce died and other people slept in the streets, he was off smiling in front of hot lights and cameras. He had to be made an example of. There was no stronger way to get my message across than if I killed him. And then I would be notorious. The world would see that the hand-truck driver was as important and capable as the rich, adored actor.

If I didn't take care of him, I would be a failure. I would be no better than him. It was a failure I couldn't live with. A failure the world would regret.

But no one would regret it as much as They would. Knock-knock went the gavel in my mind upstairs. 'Raymond Tompkins. Guilty as charged.' It took five of Their little child hands to lift the gavel. More like a sledgehammer than a gavel, really, so it was understandable.

Now that I had plans, I felt I could face Marta. Marta could have been a savior to me, but she entered a bad moral neighborhood and seemed to like it there. She set up permanent residence. I could face her now because I didn't need her anymore. I had a new savior, my determination. I had found something that would love me back. I sat at the table by the window, my new gun in hand, inspecting it, and called her. The gun looked nice. Almost smiling at me like a happy rookie. The phone rang three times. She was home.

'Hey, Marta,' I said.

'Ray?'

'Yes.'

'God, Ray, why haven't you called me?'

'You haven't called me either,' I said.

'Well.'

'How are you?'

'Me? I'm OK. Robbie is back living with me. He didn't like living with his father. He said he got bored.'

'Yeah?'

'Yeah. It's nice to have him around again. He'll be leaving soon, though. He's going to college in the fall. It's only a community college but he's going to try and get a place of his own.'

'That's good.'

'Yeah. Ray, are you OK? You sound down.'

'Me? I'm OK. I'm better than I have been in a while.'

'Really? That's good.' I could hear her shuffling papers as if I'd called her at the office. I thought I could sense her reading. 'Are you seeing anyone?' she asked. 'Are you seeing that woman you took to the party?'

'You sound like my mother. My mother asks questions like that.'

'What else is there to talk about?'

I thought about that. 'I don't know. Anyway, she's dead.'

'Who? The woman from the party?'

I almost said, 'No, my mother,' but I decided to tell the truth. Even if it was bad truth. I said, 'Yeah, her.'

'What happened?'

'She got beat up.'

'Really? By who?' She was shocked.

'Her ex-boyfriend.'

'What? Jesus.'

'How about your love life?'

'Mine? Well, you know.'

'No.'

'Don't ask me about this, Ray.'

'I told you,' I said, 'now you tell me.'

'Well, me and Bill broke up.'

'Broke up, huh?' For some reason, the news didn't make me happy.

'Yeah,' she said. 'He started sleeping with other girls. He even slept with that pretty girl you brought to the party. Can you believe that?'

I believed it.

'So, he was fucking all these women and I didn't even know about it. Usually you can sense these things. But, Bill, he's so fucking cocksure all the time, who could know the difference?'

She was getting angrier and angrier. I could tell that she had told this story a lot of times. Probably mostly to herself.

'The final straw was that he gave that receptionist position to some twenty-two-year-old with a cunt as wide as his fist.' She took a breath. 'Goddamn, I'm bitter about it. You know?'

'I know.'

'Yeah. So, now I'm alone.' She paused. 'I feel good about it,' she told herself. 'Do you want to come over?'

'No.'

'Why not?'

'I'm better off being alone too.'

'Yeah? Well. Are you sure?'

'Yes,' I said.

'I'd like to see you. What have you been doing with yourself?'

'I've been doing things. Good things.'

'Like what?'

'It doesn't matter. You'll know soon.'

She was quiet.

'I hope you're doing OK,' she said.

'I'm doing fine. I've finally found a purpose.'

'Yeah?'

'I've lived my whole life without a purpose. I was passionless, Marta. Going nowhere. No focus. Do you know what it's like to be passionless?'

'Sure, I know.'

She knew. We used to feel that way together.

'Well, I've finally found my way. I'm finally doing something right.'

'What is it?'

'It doesn't matter.'

'It doesn't? I'd like to know.'

'No. It will be so obvious to you soon that there's no point in telling you. All I can say is it's important. It will change the world.'

'Well . . . OK.' She didn't know what to say.

'I've got to go, Marta.'

'Are you sure you don't want to come over?'

'Yeah.'

'I wish you would. I miss you, Ray,' she said.

'I've got something I have to do.'

'I've been bad off lately, Ray. That thing with Bill sometimes makes me want to kill.'

'I can understand,' I said.

Chapter Twenty-two

.38 CALIBER PERFORMANCE

THE DAY OF the première.

I went to the library to check the day's *Variety*. The same librarian was there who always helped me but gave me sour, scolding looks.

The front page headline talked about a merger between two studios. A story about Griffith was on page six.

'The première of Tim Griffith's new movie, *The Lesser of Two Evils*, is going on tonight at the Avco theater in Westwood. Buzz from the early première in New York says that Griffith gives an "Oscar Caliber Performance." The eagerly anticipated film co-stars Melanie Moore and James Nyves. The director, Brian Alexander, will not be at the première because he is directing a new film in the Philippines.'

I'm going to get you Griffith, I thought. For everything you represent. I'll give you a performance worthy of an award. I'll kill you with my Oscar Caliber Gun.

I drove from the library to the Avco theater in Westwood. I had seen movies there before. The screens were big. All the blockbuster movies played there. I once waited four hours in the heat to see *Star Wars*. A solid line of restless, obsessed fans, sunburned but happy.

I checked the layout of the theater. Outside there was a wide sidewalk between the theater and a few restaurants across the way. The sidewalk led to a parking lot in back. There was no way for me to tell how the première was going to be set up, but I figured that the limos would pull up to the curb in the front of the theater and the stars would walk along the wide sidewalk to the side entrance. In that case, I could stand by one of the potted plants along the sidewalk and see everything. I stood at a potted plant and watched the sidewalk for a minute. I just imagined what it would be like later. Swarms of people, first happy and excited, then screaming and chaotic. Right now, a few couples were sitting outside at the restaurants eating. The theater looked deserted.

I walked up and down the alley next to the theater. There wasn't much I could do now. I had to wait until later.

I went back home. I sat down at my desk in the living room like I had when I wrote all the letters and I wrote another one. It would be my last letter. It was two o'clock. Six hours away.

If you are reading this then you know who I am and I have done what I set out to do. I want the world to know that Tim Griffith is not what he appears to be. He is all polish. He has gotten by on his pretty smile. But he doesn't know anything about people like me. People who suffer, people who wade through disappointment, people who have to work hard jobs. Tim Griffith doesn't understand what it's like to be a real person. He lives in a beach house with three buildings and a Bel-Air home which looks like a fortress behind a black gate.

Millions of people adore this man. But he doesn't understand the lives of the people who adore him. And he keeps making movies so his adoring public will grow. He is pure ego. He is everything bad about this screwed up place we call the world. He gets by with easy good looks while others suffer.

His movies are the same way, out-of-touch. They propagate bad morals and bad ideas. But people go on loving this man. Tim Griffith is the Golden Calf. He is a false idol. He destroys this world we live in by showing that a smile and pretty eyes are better than anything. People must know that their devotion to this man is wrong because he represents terrible things — shallowness and brutality.

So, you who are reading this now know the truth. Tim

*Griffith had to be stopped. He must be made an example.
If I die in the process then that's OK. The job is important
enough. I'll have changed the world.*

Raymond Walter Tompkins

I took my birth certificate out of the desk drawer and laid it on
the desk next to the letter. I didn't want there to be any confusion
about who I was.

I read the letter once over. It was satisfactory. It was short
but it made my point. It told everything I wanted to tell. I read
it again and set down the pen on the desk next to the letter. I
put four solid prints on the pen so they would know exactly who
wrote the letter.

I stared at the wall. Paint was peeling in flakes. The première
was hours away.

I wanted to call Marta one last time. If I talked to anybody for
the last time, it would be her. I had to admit, through everything
that had happened in recent months, I still liked her. She was an
example of how the world took a sweet seed and made it bitter.
Even though she ignored me and didn't return my affection, I
believed she was a decent person. She was an example of how
the world itself was the bad seed. It turned good people bad.
That didn't make it any easier to see her with Bill or feel her
rejection, but it made it easier to hunt Griffith. You see, Griffith
planted the world's bad seed. He was a lucky devil who glorified
straight teeth, diamond-cut chin, smiling eyes and pink lips, while
the toothless and hare-lipped, or even the pretty but poor, prayed
to God, or maybe to actors and sports stars, and tried to live
with their own misery, a misery planted by the actor himself in
his movies and his magazine covers. Hell of a fucking paradox.

When I called Marta, I got her machine. 'This is Marta. Leave
a message or call me back.' The machine beeped. 'Marta, this is
Ray, I—' She picked up.

'Ray.'

'Are you screening calls, Marta?'

'Yeah,' she said.

'Why?'

'Bill's been calling me.'

'Oh.'

'How are you, Ray?'

She sounded nervous, as if she was being watched. I gave her my heavy statements anyway.

'I've called to say good-bye,' I said.

'Good-bye? Where are you going?'

'I've got a job to do.'

'Is it out-of-state?'

'You could say that,' I said.

'What is it?'

'I can't say.'

'Where, Ray? I wish you'd tell me.'

'All I can say is that there is something very evil and it needs to be killed.' I hadn't put it so well, so concisely, yet.

'What do you mean?' She was upset. She shrieked those last words.

'Nothing. I don't mean anything.'

'I'm worried about you, Ray. I've been thinking about the last conversation we had. You sounded so down. Please come over.'

'I can't do that. Don't worry. You don't have anything to worry about. In fact, you can look forward to a better world.'

'Ray, you're not going to do something, are you?'

'No,' I said. 'Of course I am,' I thought. In my head, there was a studio audience 'Yahoo!'

I said, 'Don't worry. I just wanted to talk to you.'

'Please come over,' she said, carefully sounding each word. 'I want to see you.'

'Not today, Marta. Some other time.'

'Are you sure?'

'Yes.'

Then she said, 'I would come over, but I have to stay here.'

'Why?'

'I'm waiting for Bill to call.'

Just the sound of his name made my gut start throbbing like my heart. And it made Them shriek something wicked. 'Eeek,' They said.

'I thought you didn't want to talk to him.'

'I don't. It's confusing.'

'Right.'

'Are you sure you don't want to come over?'

'Yes.' I stopped, looked at my letter sitting on the desk. 'I wanted to call because I like you, Marta. I wanted you to know that.'

'I know that.'

'I really like you, Marta. We could have had something, if you didn't go out with that fucking guy, Bill. I'm a decent person, Marta, and you just couldn't see it.'

'I'm sorry about that, Ray.'

'I'm sorry too.'

'Maybe we can make something of it now.'

'No. That's not possible. I just wanted to talk to you one more time.'

'What?' She was sad and distressed. 'I like you, Ray. Please remember that. A lot of people like you.'

'All right. Bye, Marta.'

'Wait, Ray. I want to—'

'I have to go.'

We said good-bye. She didn't want to get off the phone. I almost had to hang up on her. 'See you,' she finally said and our friendship was over.

It was six o'clock. I was getting restless. I needed to kill time. I found the number for the payphone outside and dialed it. A man wearing a straw hat picked up.

'I know where you live,' I said.

'You do?'

'I know where you live and I watch you.'

'Now, how could you know where I live, if I just picked up at random?'

I hung up. Smart fuck. He walked away smiling to himself. I dialed again. A woman picked up, young and glowing.

'Tonight is the night when I kill you.'

She took the phone away from her ear and looked at it. She walked away, then turned it into a sprint. The phone was left dangling on its silver cord.

The première was an hour and a half away, but I wanted to get there early to find a good spot.

I got there very early. The place was mostly empty. Pretty people in red and white uniforms were laying down a red carpet. Some other people were setting up a twenty-foot buffet table in the parking lot behind the theater. The gun was in the right front pocket of my baggy green pants. I held it with one hand.

I walked back to the parking lot. A security guard came up to me immediately and said, 'You can't be here.' He stared at me hard until I left. I still held the gun in my pocket. It was probably the most exciting thing the security guard had to do all day.

I walked back to the theater. I stood against the theater wall and spent the next hour watching everything unfold.

A man walked up to me. He was round and pale and looked like his only source of light was television. He held something that looked like a brochure in his puffy, pink hand. It was a folded picture of Tim Griffith. I could see Griffith's blue eyes and parted hair.

'Are you here for the première?' he asked.

'Yes.'

'So am I.'

He paused and watched the people working.

'I've come to most of Tim Griffith's premières,' he said. 'I love watching the stars. I'm looking forward to this movie. The New

York reviewer gave it a great review. I hope to get an autograph.'
He held up the picture.

I didn't say anything.

'They're setting up a whole party out back. They're giving away promotional souvenirs. I've seen the box that they're handing out. I'm not sure what's inside but I'd sure like to get my hands on one of them.'

I walked away from him without saying anything. He didn't call after me. I leaned against an office-building wall next to a restaurant. The pudgy, pink man remained near the theater, watching everybody work. Occasionally he gave a sad, confused glance my way.

Soon, the velvet ropes were up, the red carpet laid down and people started arriving. The press who had television cameras went back into the parking lot. The press who were taking photographs stayed by the ropes. Fans and passersby stayed in a crowd on either side of the red carpet. The theater employees stood in their brown and white uniforms on the theater steps. Ten Playboy playmates arrived wearing bow ties around their necks and bushy white tails. They stood at the entrance to the parking lot and began handing out the boxes of souvenirs and hats which said the name of the movie. The première was larger than I thought it would be.

I figured there would be extra security. Griffith might have told them about me. And he probably gave the police a description after I met him at the set. But who was I? I was a male in his late twenties. I looked less like a criminal than some of the photographers.

Famous and important people walked along the red carpet under the hot lights and flashing cameras. The lights were bright like those of a stage or at a nighttime sporting event. The celebrities all looked smug and proud, waving to the spotlight, a constant look like they were being televised. They smiled out with false, full-toothed smiles and unfocused stares, not looking anyone straight in the eye. They almost seemed sad and trapped, like zoo animals.

I leaned against a potted tree. It was a miniature pine. I could see everything. The tree cleared a small space so there was a gap in the crowd. I tapped at the gun with one finger like I was twiddling my thumbs. I didn't care about the other celebrities. I was waiting for Tim Griffith and Robin Culver. So was everybody else.

A limo pulled up, front and center, and they walked out. The crowd talked a low murmur. Some people called out their names. Robin Culver was heavily pregnant, wearing an orange, flowery maternity dress. She was smiling. Griffith was wearing a black suit and a black tie. He was a few inches shorter than her. A strand of hair fell on his forehead. She walked on the right side of him, on my side. That would make it harder for me to get to Griffith. They were ten feet away. He was smiling. He looked happy.

They were almost to me. Five feet, four feet, right in front of me. Griffith was waving. His hand fell when I shot him. All my anger came out the end of that gun.

I thought I got him twice. Once in the side and once on the arm. As soon as the shots were fired, I had an instant sense of relief and relaxation. Almost a sense of calm pride, mixed with elation. I shot quick and aimed for his head. His hand went up to his ear. Time was moving slow enough so that I thought, 'Damn, I missed his head but maybe I took off an ear. And who's going to watch an actor without an ear.'

His wife ducked and fell. He fell left. His eyes tilted into his head. The blood ran out of his face and he didn't look pretty anymore. People screamed. It wouldn't matter what happened to me now. Four fans jumped on me. My arm fell hard against the potted tree. I felt it crack. No one said anything but I saw four angry faces falling towards my own. My last thought was that this was what it must be like to try and shoot the President. My head hit the pavement. I blacked out.

Chapter Twenty-three

THE END

'WHY DID YOU do this?' the psychiatrist asked me. He was a young guy in his thirties. No beard. He didn't look like he should be a psychiatrist. Two cops stood by. We were in a small white room.

'I felt Tim Griffith should be stopped.'

'Why?'

'He lives in his beach house and his Bel-Air mansion while people like me are poor and miserable.'

'So you resented him for his wealth.'

'It's more than that. People love Tim Griffith. He lives on a pedestal but he doesn't understand real life and real people.'

'You resent him for his fame, then.'

'No. I felt he was getting away with murder.'

'That's very funny.'

'I wanted to show people that he was a false idol. He was corrupt.'

'So you felt you needed to shoot him?'

'That was the only way to really show people right and wrong.'

'Don't you think it's wrong to kill a person?'

'He is one person. He has an effect on millions of people. The effect he has on people is far more dangerous than me killing one man.'

He wrote something on a notepad.

'Griffith shouldn't be allowed to live so well when others have so little.'

'The wealth, you mean?'

'Yes.'

'Are you a socialist?'

'A socialist?'

'Yes, do you think there should be equal wealth for everybody.'

'I don't know about that. I don't have any political affiliations.'

'No?'

'No. I go by my own policy.'

'So you wanted to show the world that Tim Griffith was a bad person.'

'Yes.'

'Do you want to see the effect you're having on people?'

'Yes.'

There was a brand new black TV with a built-in VCR in the room. The psychiatrist motioned to one of the cops and he turned on the TV.

'You're on every station, did you know that?'

'No.'

The psychiatrist switched through a couple of stations until he landed on a network. A pretty blonde news reporter with heavy make-up was standing in front of my apartment building. The word 'Live' was in the corner of the screen.

'. . . joining us. The man, now disclosed as,' she looked down, 'Raymond Walter Tompkins, was apartment manager in this building behind me. Apparently, he left what seems to be a suicide note inside the apartment. In the note, he refers to Griffith as a "Golden Calf" and was upset with Griffith's wealth and fame. He says, and here I quote, "Tim Griffith is the Golden Calf. He is a false idol. He destroys this world we live in by showing that a smile and pretty eyes are better than anything." In his apartment, police found copies of Tim Griffith's movies and many articles on the actor. They did not find any other weapons besides the gun he used at the première. Tim Griffith is in fair condition at a Westwood hospital. We know he has gunshot wounds to his side, his face and his right arm, but that is all we have been told. We will bring more information as it unfolds.'

The psychiatrist turned down the volume. 'Do you see what has happened?' he said.

'Yes.'

'It is a tragedy.'

'Yes, it is.'

'People do not love a tragedy.'

'They will understand when they hear the contents of my note.'

'I've read your note.'

'Have you?'

'I don't think people will understand.'

'Sure they will.'

'Why?'

'People love to follow a good story. Right there on TV they said twice as much about me as they did about Tim Griffith. They will be watching about me around the clock.'

'That's not saying anything.'

'That's saying that all the news programs will have stories about me. They will interview my parents. There will be segments about my childhood. People are going to watch to see who I am and they are going to be sympathetic.'

'I doubt it, Mr Tompkins.'

'Don't underestimate how much the public likes to adore people.'

'I'm not.'

'Like cattle.'

'Don't you feel any regret for having tried to kill a man?'

'I'm all over TV. What do I have to regret?'

They walked me down a white, linoleum corridor. I didn't know where I was. After I fired the bullets and blacked out, I was unconscious the whole night. Maybe out of shock. There was a temporary bandage on my arm. My arm was broken. woke up in jail.

They took me to my cell.

'Can I have a TV?' I asked.

'No,' said one of the cops. He looked down at me like he wanted to beat me right there.

The cop looked at the psychiatrist. 'He has all these letters coming in. What should I do with them?'

He handed the psychiatrist a large white envelope. 'These are just the ones that were hand-delivered.' The psychiatrist looked inside. He opened up a letter and read it. 'I'll let him have these. He is going to be in there quite a while. Maybe these letters will teach him something.' He handed me the envelope. 'Wait,' he said. He took back the envelope and ripped off the metal peg used to seal the envelope down. 'OK.'

They put me inside the cell and closed the door. The cell was a small room with a bed, a metal sink and a toilet.

I sat on the bed and opened the white envelope. The psychiatrist must have thought all those letters were hate mail. He was wrong. The letter he picked up must have been hate mail, but the other ones were different.

Dear Ray,
    I just heard your letter read on the news. I understand what you're saying. I have always wondered about celebrities myself. They live so high and mighty but they don't understand a thing about real people like you and me. You are a smart man.

Another one.

Dear Mr Tompkins,
    I am watching you. Ha! Just kidding. I wish I was in there watching you and comforting you. You deserve it. I am a housewife with two daughters and a husband who doesn't know anything. He's mean as well. Not like you. You're good, I can

*u see through all the bullshit that goes on in the world
my language). Tim Griffith is all polish, like you
'e gets by on good looks and nothing else. That kind of
g should be stopped. I'm glad you were there to try.*

t new friend,
Dawson

mail letter.

ar stupid,
*How could you try to kill a man who entertains and brings good
eeling to so many people. What have you ever done for anybody?
I hope you get the gas chamber. I am seventy-six and I have been
watching Tim Griffith's career from the beginning. I don't know
what I would have done if you killed him. I may have come over
there and killed you myself. I hope you rot. You are a sick asshole.
Your parents deserve to die for giving birth to a demon like you.
Martha Graves
Riverside*

My favorite letter was four pages long and ended with this
paragraph:

*I am watching TV and it makes my eyes burn what they
say about you. They are vilifying you. They say you are a
"Troubled man." What they don't know is that you are more
together than everyone. I love you, Mr Tompkins. I know you
have not received much love your entire life but now you have
won my love. You have won the hearts of millions. They know
who you are now, Mr Tompkins, and they understand. You
are going to live in the minds of people forever as the man who
tried to change things for the better. Tim Griffith is all good
looks, and nothing that you or me feel. You are the leader of
a worthy cause. Congratulations.*